# I Am Missing

Gemini Series, Book 3

By

Ty Patterson

## Books by Ty Patterson

<u>Warriors Series Shorts</u>

*This is a series of novellas that link to the Warriors Series thrillers*

*Zulu Hour*, Warriors Series Shorts, Book 1 (set before *The Warrior*)
*The Watcher*, Warriors Series Shorts, Book 2 (set between *The Warrior* and *The Warrior Code*)
*The Shadow*, Warriors Series Shorts, Book 3 (set before *The Warrior*)
*The Man From Congo*, Warriors Series Shorts, Book 4
Warriors Series Shorts, Boxset I, Books 1-4
*The Texan*, Warriors Series Shorts, Book 5
*The Heavies*, Warriors Series Shorts, Book 6

<u>Gemini Series</u>

*Dividing Zero*, Gemini Series, Book 1
*Defending Cain*, Gemini Series, Book 2
*I Am Missing*, Gemini Series, Book 3

<u>Warriors Series</u>

*The Warrior*, Warriors series, Book 1
*The Reluctant Warrior*, Warriors series, Book 2
*The Warrior Code*, Warriors series, Book 3
*The Warrior's Debt*, Warriors series, Book 4
*Flay*, Warriors series, Book 5
*Behind You*, Warriors series, Book 6
*Hunting You*, Warriors series, Book 7
*Zero*, Warriors series, Book 8
*Death Club*, Warriors series, Book 9
*Trigger Break*, Warriors series, Book 10
*Scorched Earth*, Warriors series, Book 11
*RUN!*, Warriors series, Book 12
Warriors series Boxset, Books 1-4
Warriors series Boxset II, Books 5-8
Warriors series Boxset III, Books 1-8

Sign up to Ty Patterson's mailing list, and get The Warrior, #1 in the USA Today Bestselling Warriors Series, free. Be the first to know about new releases and deals.

Check out Ty on Amazon, on iTunes, on Kobo and on Barnes and Noble.

# Acknowledgments

No book is a single person's product. I am privileged that *I Am Missing* has benefited from the input of several great people.

Sylvia Foster, Cary Lory Becker, Charlie Carrick, Pat Ellis, Dori Barrett, Simon Alphonso, Dave Davis, V. Elizabeth Perry, Ann Finn, Pete Bennett, Eric Blackburn, Margaret Harvey, David Hay, Jim Lambert, Terry Pellman, Jimmy Smith, Theresa, and Mark Campbell, who are my beta readers and who helped shape my book, my launch team for supporting me, Eliza Dee and Dawn Nassise for their editing, and Donna Rich for her proofreading.

# Dedications

To Michelle Rose Dunn, Debbie Bruns Gallant, and Cheri Gerhardt, for supporting me.

To all the men and women in uniform who make it possible for us to enjoy our freedom.

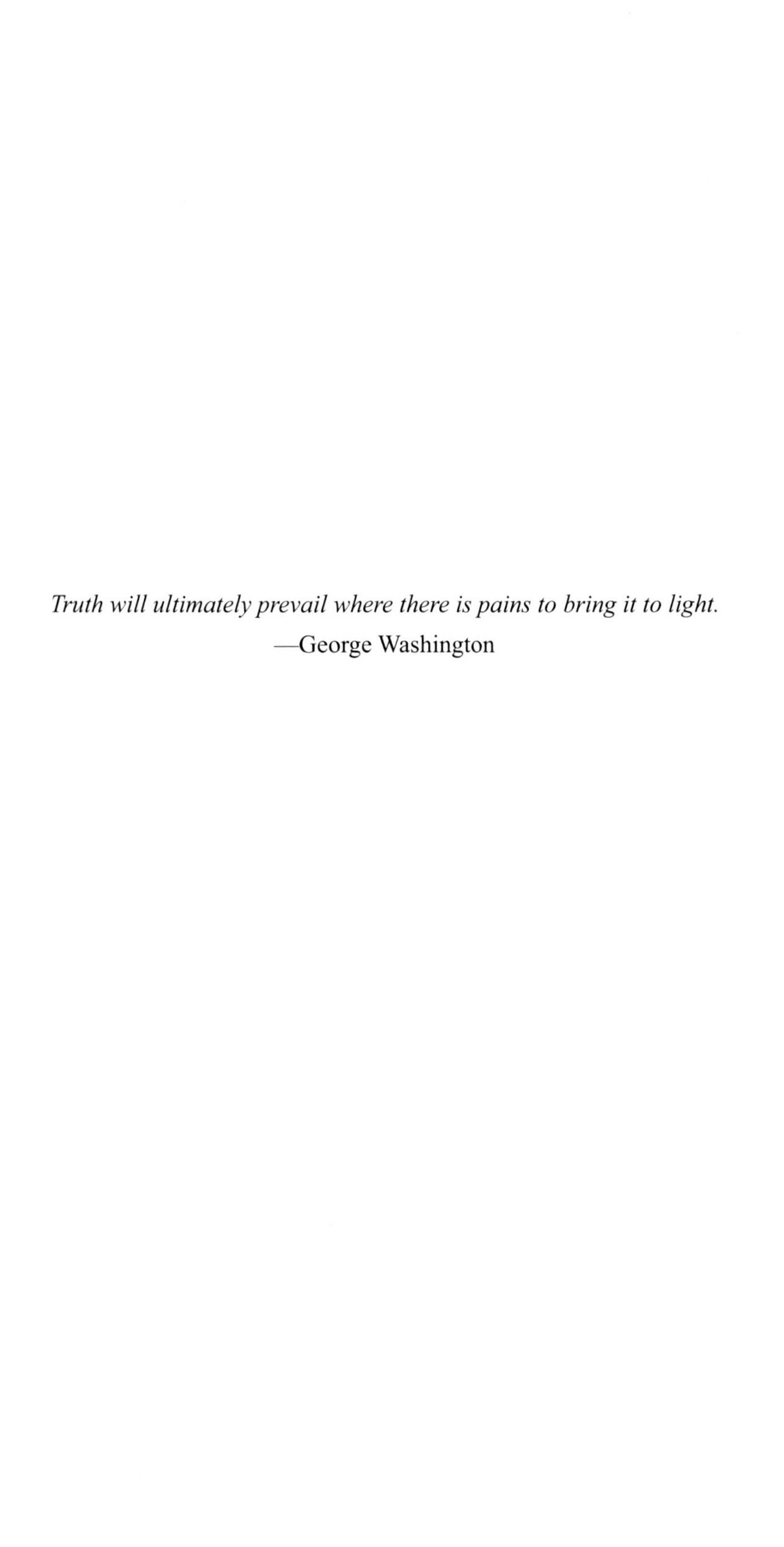

*Truth will ultimately prevail where there is pains to bring it to light.*

—George Washington

# Chapter 1

As days went, there was nothing special about this particular one.

Beth and Meghan Petersen were at their screens in their Columbus Avenue office, working on the logistics of a mission.

There wasn't anything burning, missionwise.

Zeb Carter, the lead agent of the clandestine outfit they worked for, was on a solo mission in the Middle East.

Broker, the intel guy in the unit, was on vacation with his girlfriend, Sarah Burke, who was high up in the FBI. Bear and Chloe, two of the operatives, were away too.

On one couch, a tall black man was sprawled out. He was large, and when he stood, he invariably dwarfed all those present. Bwana was six feet four, muscled, and yet moved like a cat.

On another couch, a blond-haired man slept. He was movie-star handsome and made a show of being a gift to womankind.

His friends knew Roger, the blond Texan, was all show. He had a girlfriend who he was deeply committed to.

The eight of them worked for the Agency. Just that, no other name.

It was a unique small-footprint outfit that dealt with terrorists, international criminal gangs, and threats to national security.

It was headed by a female director, Clare, no last name. She was based out of D.C. and reported to only one person. The president.

Of course, the Agency didn't advertise itself. It didn't exist, not on paper or in any other record.

All of them worked for a security consulting firm that advised corporations on people and perimeter protection.

The firm was a front. They had real clients and genuinely advised them, but it still was a façade.

For such a small unit, they were very well resourced. That was courtesy of generous rewards from grateful Middle Eastern royalty they had helped.

Like that building on Columbus Avenue. They owned it outright.

Then there was that Gulfstream. They owned that one too.

Werner, a highly sophisticated artificial intelligence program, they owned outright. The software resided in a supercomputer in their office and was the envy of the NSA and a few other intelligence agencies. They used the name Werner loosely, to refer either to the program or to the machine.

They possessed a fleet of vehicles—SUVs, armored, equipped with run-flats and stealth paint, more gadgets and tech in them than the Batmobile had.

The twins were the only ones who didn't have an Army background. Zeb, Bwana, Roger, and Bear were former Special Forces operatives.

Broker was an ex-Ranger, a higher life form, he declared. Chloe had been with the Eighty-Second Airborne.

Zeb was an odd one. He rarely smiled and hardly spoke. He was single, didn't date, and had no interest in romantic entanglements.

Despite his peculiarities, there was something about him. He was the reason the Agency worked. He was their leader, but he didn't do all that command stuff.

He was a friend, first and foremost, and that just suited the rest of them.

The day dragged on as some days did.

Beth yawned and glanced at her watch.

'Mark's coming?' her sister asked. They weren't just sisters, they were twins, Meghan the elder one.

Brown-haired, green-eyed, vivacious, sassy, beautiful—a newspaper had once devoted a page length of adjectives to describe them. This was after a mission had made them into celebrities.

'Yeah, what about you? You still dating that Wall Street guy?'

'Nah.' Meghan stretched. 'I'm out of the dating scene.'

Mark was Beth's significant other. A cop in the NYPD. The two were close, very close. Everyone approved.

Beth rose to make them coffee when the phone rang.

She quirked an eyebrow as she listened silently.

'Send them up,' she replied and hung up.

'Who was it?'

'You'll see.'

Four men entered their office through the elevator.

In the front were two large men, as large as Bwana, but these two had none of his grace.

They had muscles, but developed in gyms and aided by the generous use of steroids.

They had short dark hair and wore well-cut suits, bulges under their jackets.

Behind them were two men, one wearing a pin-striped suit, carrying a briefcase, while the other was more casually dressed.

He was blond, tieless, blue jacket over white shirt, blue jeans, and brown shoes.

'Beth and Meghan Petersen?' Pinstripe halted and looked in their direction.

'That's us,' Meghan answered and gestured at a few seats.

The heavies, for that was who they were, stood silently as Pinstripe and Blue Jacket seated themselves.

'I'm Ken Farrell,' Pinstripe introduced himself. 'And this is—'

'We know who he is,' Meghan said drily.

Cole Patten, Blue Jacket, was a billionaire. He was in his late thirties and had inherited a steel empire when he was young, very young.

He had built on his inheritance and multiplied it several times. He was frequently in the news, and not always for the right reasons.

There were frequent rumors that his business dealings were shady and that he had links to criminal gangs.

He dated Hollywood actresses and models, and his social life was avidly covered by the gossip magazines.

Farrell looked around him before settling his eyes on the twins. 'I expected a bigger office. More people.'

Neither of the sisters responded. They knew each other well and often could read one another's mind.

Farrell cleared his throat in the silence and smiled a warm smile. One that said, *I am your best friend.* The sisters immediately distrusted him.

'We want to hire you.'

'And you are?' Beth asked him bluntly.

'I'm sorry, I should have explained. I'm Cole's lawyer.'

'We are not for hire, Mr. Farrell,' she cut him off. Mark would arrive soon. Beth wanted the visitors out as quickly as possible.

'Why don't you hear us out, ma'am?'

'Sorry, not interested. I let you in just to see what a billionaire looked like and who he moved around with. A lawyer and two heavies. We've seen our fill. Besides, there's all those rumors about the legality of Patten's businesses. Not to our liking. There's the elevator. Thank you.'

Farrell made to speak but kept quiet when Patten laid a hand on his shoulder.

'I came to you because I have a particular problem.' His voice was pleasant, his eyes warm. 'One that I think you can help with, given that you are twins.'

'What's that?'

'I am missing. I want you to find me.'

# Chapter 2

'You're missing?' Beth twirled a pencil in her fingers, her face giving nothing away.

Ken Farrell nodded. 'It's like this—'

'Not you,' she cut him off. 'Let *him* explain.'

Farrell's expression didn't change. Either he was a highly experienced lawyer, or he had a thick skin.

*Both. A billionaire doesn't hire cheapos.*

'What do you know of me?' Cole Patten gave them a searching look.

'Assume we know nothing.'

The steel magnate nodded and began.

Cole and Josh, twins, had been born to Rachel and Billy Patten, thirty-eight years back, in Chisholm, Minnesota.

Their father was a Vietnam vet, and on his return from the war, he had bought an iron ore mine near their hometown.

Rachel's family owned a chain of motels and hotels in the state. They'd loaned Billy Patten the seed money, five million, to buy the failing mine. Funds that he had repaid several times over.

Billy Patten was smart, hardworking, and a charmer. He cajoled and coaxed, threatened and negotiated, and turned the mine around. Once it was profitable, he bought another. And then another. By the time the brothers were seven years old, he had grown the steel business into a large empire.

'It was then that he took us to Vietnam,' Cole Patten reminisced.

Beth remembered some of the headlines but kept quiet, letting their visitor tell his story.

'We were young. Seven. All we knew was that our dad was a hero. He never spoke of the war. Mom? She died when we were two. Don't remember much of her. Dad brought us up by himself. He had some help from Mom's sister, Ginny Davis, but not much. Mom's side of the family wasn't that close.'

'What happened in Vietnam?' Meghan reminded him.

'Vietnam? The war defined Dad. It shaped him. It gave him the drive. He would say if it hadn't been for the war, he wouldn't have been a businessman. He took both of us to Ho Chi Minh City. And from there, to Cu Chi.'

Cu Chi. Beth exchanged a glance with her sister. The place was synonymous with underground tunnels that the Viet Cong had built. It was in those dark, deep passages that they had waged a savage war against the American, Australian, and New Zealand forces.

'Your father was a Tunnel Rat?'

'Yes. He wanted us to see that country. Show where he had been. He took us to one of the tunnels. You might have read of this…' He trailed off.

Beth made a *carry on* gesture with her hand and Patten nodded.

'He took us to one of the restricted areas. The tunnel was

weak in that area. Walls were crumbling. It collapsed on us. I fainted. Next thing I remember, I was in the hospital, and Dad and Josh were dead.'

Bwana shifted on his couch but didn't speak. No one uttered a word until Patten resumed.

'Farrell's law firm was representing us. Has been the family and business law firm for years. They made all the arrangements. I returned. Inherited the steel business. There was a hotel chain too. That would have gone to Josh.'

'I don't recall a hotel business being mentioned'—Beth narrowed her eyes—'whenever your name comes up.'

Patten smiled. 'That's because it's still in a trust. I have nothing to do with it. I run the Chisholm Corporation, which is in steel. It, too, was in a trust until I turned eighteen.'

'You took it public a while back. Expanded. Bought mines and operations across the world. Chisholm is what, the second- or third-largest steel business in the world?'

'It's in the top five,' Patten replied self-deprecatingly.

'You're a billionaire.' Beth ticked off on her fingers. 'You're single. You own one of the largest businesses in the world. You're well-protected.' She nodded at the goons standing silently. 'And you seem to have good advice.' Her lips curled in the lawyer's direction.

'What's gone wrong in your heaven?'

'A year back, a Russian business reached out to us and made an offer for the business. I refused. Selling wasn't in our plans, and the price was low.'

'So?'

'So, this year, a few months back, they launched a hostile takeover. They've started buying stock. Not just that, they've started playing dirty.'

'How?'

'Billy Patten's will was specific,' Farrell stepped in, his voice dry and precise. 'In the event of his death, Cole was to inherit the steel business, while the hotel chain would go to Josh.

'But Josh is dead,' Beth exclaimed, 'What has happened to the hotels business?'

'It is managed by the trust.'

Farrell waited for a moment and when there were no further questions, resumed.

'The Russian firm is claiming that Cole Patten isn't who he is. They say Cole died in Vietnam. The man in front of you is Josh Patten, according to them.'

The sisters gaped at the lawyer for a few seconds. 'What? That should be easy to prove, shouldn't it?'

'I wish it was.' Farrell allowed a grimace to appear on his face. 'There are no DNA records. No fingerprints. No hair samples. No distinguishing marks that tell one twin from the other. Nothing remains of Josh Patten. Even if it did, there's nothing to conclusively say this is Cole and the sibling who died was Josh.'

'What about you? Surely you knew the brothers.'

'No, ma'am. My father used to handle Billy Patten and Chisholm's affairs in those days. I met Cole for the first time when my father arranged for him to be brought back from Vietnam. My father died soon after that, and I stepped in.'

'Your dad? Surely he confirmed Cole Patten's identity?'

'Not explicitly. His health was failing. He was in the hospital. His people did all the work. He met the boy just a few times, and then Cole went into counseling and therapy. My father never recovered and didn't meet Cole subsequently.'

'What about Billy Patten and Rachel's families?'

'Billy was an only child. Rachel's sister, Ginny, is still alive. However, she wasn't close the Pattens and she couldn't identify the twins. We checked. Billy and Rachel's parents dead. There's no one left on Billy's side. There are a few other relatives on Rachel's side, but they are distant. None of them could tell the boys apart.'

'What about birth records?'

'They don't prove anything. They have just names, dates and not much else. There is no way to prove that Cole's certificate is his. Cole is elder by a few minutes, that's all we know.'

'What about friends?'

'No friends to identify them. Cole Patten lived in New York after his return from Vietnam. This is his home now. He lost contact with the friends he grew up with. We reached out to a few, and they couldn't prove anything.'

'It's his word against the Russian company's.' He sighed heavily.

'I don't believe this.' Beth smacked her palm on her table. 'These guys just waltz in and say Mr. Patten isn't who he is? And there's nothing to prove otherwise?'

'We've run the brothers' photographs through sophisticated aging programs. Shown them to the Russian firm's lawyers. They aren't convinced. They put up photographs of their own. It's our word against theirs. Doesn't cut much ice.'

'In the meantime,' the billionaire took over from his lawyer, 'Chisholm Corporation's share price has tanked. It's reduced the company's value. My board is unhappy. They want me to clear this matter up. Fast.'

'How much of the company do you own?' Meghan asked curiously.

'Thirty percent.'

'What happens if you turn out to be Josh Patten?'

'The company will take over my ownership. There are specific conditions under which they can do so. This is one of them. But that's not the end of it. I'll be liable for criminal charges. For impersonating my brother. A whole world of trouble will open up.'

'Are you Josh Patten?' She looked him in the eye.

'No, ma'am.'

'Why us? You're a billionaire. You can hire the best investigators. I'm sure the NYPD would help you.'

'You have something none of them do.' Cole Patten smiled thinly. 'You're twins.'

'Why did you say you were missing?'

'My father and Josh—their bodies were never found.

'They're still missing. Presumed dead.'

# Chapter 3

Meghan rose and paced the room, a disbelieving look on her face. 'Some Russian dude has accused you of not being you. Your father and brother are missing. There's no way to prove your identity. You have any other surprises for us?'

'So, you're going to take my case?' Patten countered with a trace of satisfaction in his voice.

'We're undecided,' she replied firmly. 'You have an interesting problem, but we have a rule of not working with criminals.'

'My client is not a criminal,' Farrell shot back, his back stiffening.

'May not be in your eyes. But we can read between the headlines. Those labor disputes that suddenly disappeared at his plants? Those few workers who brought a suit against him and abruptly faded away? All those rumors that Patten uses strong-arm tactics? They didn't come out of nowhere, did they?'

'They didn't,' Farrell said stiffly. 'They were planted. Mr. Patten hasn't broken the law, not once. He doesn't even have a speeding ticket. You're making baseless allegations.'

Meghan snorted inelegantly. 'Why would he, when he has a chauffeur? And in this great city of ours that worships wealth, which cop would dare to issue him a ticket?'

Patten, who had been leaning back and watching the byplay with an amused smile, chuckled. 'I told Ken you were the right people to help me. He wanted to go through a large firm. I'd followed your careers. All those articles and series on you. Knew you wouldn't be awed by my status. You've proven me right.'

'That's supposed to flatter us, Mr. Patten?' The North Pole couldn't have been colder than Meghan's voice. 'You're right. Your wealth means nothing to us. We don't even like you. If we help you, it'll be because the case interests us, not you.'

'Twins. Think alike.' Beth snapped her fingers when Patten and Farrell turned to her as if seeking her opinion.

A couch creaked, Roger rising from it to pad silently into the kitchen. Bwana lay where he was, watching, listening, his body relaxed, his face expressionless.

'Those two your heavies? I guess you need a couple, going by all that happened to you.' Farrell jerked his head in the blond man's direction.

The sisters had become well known, nationally and internationally, when they had been abducted in New York. They had ended up in Syria, in the hands of terrorists, before being rescued. On their return, they had found themselves the center of media attention.

Interviews with them had run on for months. A TV channel had created a fictional series loosely based on them.

A Hollywood production house had gotten them to support a woman-directed movie that had become a worldwide blockbuster.

The attention had diminished as the media machine latched onto other public figures, but there were still times when they got recognized and a crowd formed around them.

They had discussed their celebrity status with Zeb and the crew. The Agency was covert. No one knew they worked for it. There was a danger that the media attention would expose the outfit.

To their astonishment, Zeb had asked them to embrace it.

'The more attention on you, the higher the risk for potential kidnappers,' he had clarified.

He didn't dissuade them from taking on investigative cases. Not when there weren't Agency missions running.

The twins were good at thinking laterally. Making connections that few others would spot. They were tenacious, had great instincts, and had successfully closed every case they had taken on.

They were special advisors to the NYPD's commissioner, and between client referrals and the work they did for the police, they got a steady stream of cases.

They turned most of them down, since Agency missions took precedence. The ones they took on were special, challenging, cases that appealed to them.

Like Cole Patten's.

Meghan could see the interest in Beth's eyes as Roger returned with a tray on which were a pot of coffee, several cups, and a plate full of cookies.

He placed it on a table and served Patten and Farrell silently.

His lips twitched when one of Patten's goons snorted contemptuously, but he didn't respond. Didn't even look up.

Bwana sat straighter on his couch, his face all hard angles

and planes. His eyes didn't flick to the bodyguards, but Meghan knew he was aware of every move they made. Every breath they took.

A phone rang. Roger answered it, murmuring softly. He looked at Beth.

*Mark?* she mouthed silently.

He nodded.

*Tell him I'll be late.*

'Your dad.' Beth bit into a cookie and closed her eyes momentarily in delight.

The cookies were made by a grandma who lived close by. She delivered a fresh batch each week. The sisters had helped her out once. So long as she was alive and able, the cookies would keep coming to Columbus Avenue.

'You said he borrowed money from his wife's family. Why didn't he go to a bank?' she asked Patten.

'He tried. They turned him down. He had no track record of business, no collateral. They saw him as high-risk. My mom's family were relatively well off. They had the hotel chain that Ken mentioned. They didn't approve of the marriage. They thought their daughter could do better than marry a soldier. However, she was still their daughter. They loaned him the money in the hope it would do her good. The mine didn't cost much. The owners were desperate to sell. Cash flow wasn't what it had once been.

'When will you decide?' He placed his cup back on the tray.

'When we're ready,' Meghan replied blandly.

'That's another reason I want you on my case.' Patten looked intently at the sisters.

'What's that?'

'I lost my memory. I don't remember anything that happened before that accident.'

# Chapter 4

*Now we know why he came to us*. Beth felt her sister's glance and nodded imperceptibly.

Several years back, in Wyoming, where they had been living, Beth had been held hostage at her college as a gunman had run berserk.

Cops had stormed the building, and in the ensuing shootout, a bullet had lodged itself in her head.

She had survived but had lost all her memory prior to the shooting. Meghan had taken care of her and had been there for her in those trying times. Her sister had helped her rebuild her life.

'Dissociative amnesia,' Patten roused her from her memories. 'That's what you have. Memory may return, or it may not. I have the same. In your case, your sister supported you. In my case, there wasn't any close family. Farrell's law firm helped. In fact, they were the only ones who helped.'

'You've done your research on us,' Beth acknowledged drily.

Her shooting had been covered widely, but it had also been a long while ago. Only someone who was interested in them would have dug up the information.

'My client didn't become a billionaire just like that,' Farrell didn't hide his pride.

'There are holes in your story, however,' Beth said sharply, leaning forward, ignoring the lawyer. 'Earlier, you said your father took you to the tunnels, to the restricted areas. You remember the tunnel collapsing. Then you were in hospital. You say you lost your memory, but you remember all that?'

'I don't,' Patten answered. 'That was what I was told, when I regained consciousness. In fact, I was found by a farmer outside the tunnel. I was dazed and confused. I don't remember that either. My memory starts from when I woke up in the hospital.'

'He is right,' Farrell confirmed, seeing the skeptical looks on the sisters' faces. 'There are police reports, newspaper coverage, and hospital records. Cole doesn't remember anything that happened before the hospital.'

'You also said your father didn't speak of the war. That you didn't remember your mother very well. You described how the war shaped Billy Patten,' Beth's eyes flashed as she questioned the billionaire.

'Ken Farrell,' Cole Patten looked at his lawyer, 'He filled in all those gaps for me. Told me the kind of person my father was. He spent weeks, days, telling me about my family. My not remembering my mother… that's true. I don't remember anything.'

Beth wasn't swayed by the smile he flashed.

'How do you know you are Cole Patten, in that case?'

'That was the first name that came out of my mouth. I responded to that name. You know how that works. You and I, we lost our earlier memory, but somehow we know our identity.'

She found herself nodding. What Patten was saying was true. She knew she was Beth Petersen. She had always known that, despite her amnesia.

They kept questioning him, however. Got him to narrate his account several times, but Patten stuck to his story.

'Look, my client has nothing to gain by lying,' Farrell broke in finally, in irritation.

*He's right*, Meghan thought. '*If* we take on your case'—Meghan pierced the billionaire with her gaze—'we want access to all those reports. We want to speak to those doctors, that hospital, the Vietnamese police. We will need to know everything. Not just about you, but also about Chisholm Corporation. We'll look into everyone associated with you. Even Mr. Farrell and his firm. You hide anything from us, you obstruct us, we walk away. We find you are Josh Patten, we'll report you to the cops. We'll actively help them take you down if you have knowingly indulged in criminal activity. Those will be our conditions. If we take you on.'

'Of course,' Patten said quietly, 'You will probably find that not many doctors, police, Vietnamese officials from those days are around. Some would have died, some would have moved out.'

'Why me? Neither I nor my firm are party to the investigation,' Farrell blustered. 'My client cannot reveal confidential Chisholm Corporation information.'

'Those are our conditions.'

'Accepted,' Patten said, silencing his lawyer with a look.

'We'll let you know in a few days.' Meghan rose, indicating the meeting was over.

Bwana and Roger joined the billionaire's party as they went down the elevator.

The car could comfortably hold ten people, but their presence made it feel small and crowded.

'I guess they need you around,' Farrell said snidely, breaking the silence.

'That was for us, sir?' Roger drawled.

'Who else?' Farrell sneered.

'You're wrong, sir. Those ladies, they're more than capable of looking after themselves. We were there just to make sure your thugs didn't break any flower vases.'

The doors opened before Farrell could reply.

Roger waggled his fingers at them as Patten led them away, the lawyer glaring at them.

'He doesn't like us.' Bwana scanned the street for threats out of habit.

'Yeah. It's not like we're going to lose sleep over it. You think they'll go for it?'

'The sisters? Yeah. I could see they were interested, even though they don't think much of Patten.'

'Should be interesting times. We'll hang around?'

'We will.'

'Discreetly.'

'Yup,' Bwana agreed. 'Beth and Meg will tear into us if they suspect anything.'

Ever since the kidnapping, the rest of the operatives had an unwritten and unspoken rule.

At least one of them would always be around the sisters,

when no missions were on the go.

The twins would rip into them if they found out, but that was a risk they were willing to take.

Bwana fished out his cell as he watched Patten and Farrell drive away. The goons didn't go with him. They ducked into an inconspicuous vehicle and kept watch on the building's entrance.

'Looks like they want to know what the twins do.' He spoke out of the side of his mouth, pretending not to notice the watchers.

His cell buzzed. An incoming text.

*Did they agree?*

*Not yet, but Rog and I feel they will.*

*You'll hang around?*

*Yeah. He's put men at the entrance.*

*I noticed. Maybe I'll pay them a visit.*

*Don't. Beth or Meg might find out. I wouldn't want to face a raging Petersen sister, let alone two of them.*

He dropped his cell in his jacket pocket and hurried to catch up with his friend, who was heading to a coffee shop.

'Where is he?' Roger queried.

Bwana shrugged. 'You know Zeb. He could be anywhere. That dude's like furniture. You could walk past him and not notice him.'

Zeb was slouching on a bench, several car lengths behind the thugs' vehicle. Shades and a ball cap concealed his face, and a loose jacket hid his lean figure.

An ice cream that he occasionally licked and a camera by his side gave him the appearance of a tourist.

He had returned from the Middle East, but hadn't come back to the office.

After the sisters' ordeal and rescue, he had reduced the time he spent in their building, trying to distance himself from the rest of the operatives.

He was a magnet for danger. He had enemies who would go to any lengths to get to him. That put his crew at risk. It didn't matter that his team knew of the danger and worked with him because they wanted to.

Beth and Meghan didn't know of his return. He had taken the rest of the operatives into his confidence, insisting despite their vehement protests that he would stay away for some time. Allow for any blowback from the Middle East mission to show itself. If it did, he would neutralize it, and only then would he show up at the office.

'Chernobyl will look like a walk in the park if Beth or Meg finds out,' Chloe had warned him.

Zeb hadn't replied. He knew. However, protecting the sisters came first.

He discreetly watched the heavies in the car. They made no attempt to look like part of the street. They darted occasional glances at the building's entrance and spoke to each other.

The thugs didn't bother him. They were close protection specialists who had been tasked with a job unfamiliar to them.

Surveillance was a specialized art. It required skill and guile, which they lacked.

It was the yellow cab ahead of their car that interested him.

The driver of that cab was reclining in his seat, a newspaper covering his face. To all appearances, he was asleep.

Zeb had strolled past the vehicle once and had noticed the tiny holes in the paper, through which the driver could see the building.

On a second pass, he had spotted the small camera jutting above the bottom of the window, pointed at the entrance.

*Who are you, friend?*

He noted the cab's number and queried Werner on his cell.

No such cab number existed, the program replied.

Zeb had spotted Patten the moment he had arrived at the building. Roger had messaged him the billionaire's purpose as he was making coffee for the visitors.

*Is the cab driver Patten's man? If so, why would he post his bodyguards too?*

Zeb gave up trying to figure it out and decided to wait and watch.

He was good at both. Those were just two of the many skills he had.

'What do you think?' Meghan asked her sister as they washed and put the cups away in a display cabinet.

'I don't like him. Don't trust him either.'

'Tell me something I don't know,' she smirked. 'I can see you're intrigued, however.'

'Yeah,' Beth admitted, 'it's a unique case. Proving who he is or isn't, when there's no proof.'

'Let's take it. It's not like we have a lot on our plate. Zeb's still away, and the rest of the team are on downtime.'

'And, we can't pass on the opportunity to mock Patten. Farrell, too,' her sister added solemnly before cracking up.

Meghan high-fived her, grabbed her jacket and put on her shoulder holster.

'We going somewhere?' Beth asked, puzzled.

'Yeah. To the cops.'

# Chapter 5

Pizaka and Chang were their contacts in the NYPD.

The two men headed a special task force that investigated high-profile crimes that often included terrorism. They were high up in the NYPD's hierarchy and had the commissioner's ear.

The Agency had helped the cops' careers by cracking several cases for them and allowing them to take the credit. The two cops had never forgotten and always helped out when they could.

That didn't mean both of them got along well with the operatives.

Chang, who was laid-back and looked as if he had just gotten out of bed, was thick with the twins.

Pizaka, however, was a different story.

The taller cop was always impeccably groomed and had become a minor celebrity after writing several books. He thought the operatives were vigilantes, and despite the help he had received, he treated them with disdain.

His attitude suited the twins. It gave them the opportunity to rib him mercilessly.

Despite Pizaka's prickly attitude, their relationship with the cops worked. They got fast-track access to NYPD resources and intel, whereas the cops got the credit for any cases the operatives closed in the city.

Meghan raced out of their building in their custom-built SUV. Black, with bulletproof glass and armored exterior, a souped-up engine under its hood.

'We're meeting Chang and Zak at One PP.' Beth clutched the roof handle tightly as her sister careened around a truck and shot forward. 'Not in heaven.'

Meghan blew hair out of her eyes, pursed her lips, and coaxed more speed out of the vehicle.

It was just past noon. The ever-present traffic parted for them as she raced down Seventh Avenue.

Until she let up and allowed the vehicle to slow down.

'What's up? I thought you were in a hurry.'

'We have a tail,' she replied tersely, her eyes flicking between the mirror and the vehicles ahead.

'Brown car, looks like a Toyota, two men in it,' she added as Beth extracted a battery-operated device from the glove compartment.

It had two lenses and projected the rear view onto a small screen.

She powered it on, raised it over her shoulder inconspicuously, and adjusted the focus without looking back, her eyes on the screen.

'It's them. The two heavies with Patten.'

No sooner had the words escaped her lips than Meghan braked hard, bringing the vehicle to a stop amidst New York's traffic.

She leaped out of the SUV, disregarding the honking and swearing as drivers swerved past them.

She ran past a truck, and another truck, and approached the Toyota.

Her Glock appeared magically as she stopped and flowed naturally into a fighting stance, her gun covering the startled goons.

'*Raise your hands!*' she commanded.

'You brandished your weapon in broad daylight, on a busy street,' Pizaka sneered at them an hour later.

The cop looked like he had stepped out of the cover of a men's magazine.

He was in a dark blue suit, white shirt, and red tie. The jacket fell straight, and his trousers' edge could cut through butter.

His hair was parted neatly, not a strand out of place.

He looked down through his ever-present shades at the twins, who were sprawled out in their chairs in a conference room at the NYPD headquarters.

'They nearly had an apoplectic fit,' Meghan chuckled, unabashed.

Three NYPD cruisers had surrounded her and the Toyota within minutes of her drawing her weapon.

She and Beth had been escorted away, as had the thugs.

Chang and Pizaka had arrived half an hour later and had cleared matters up with the cops. They had then driven the twins back to OnePP.

'Those cops could have shot you,' Pizaka scowled. 'It's not a laughing matter. Shots fired on a New York street!' He shuddered delicately.

'And if you had been wounded, or killed'—a horrified look crossed his face—'your friends would have gone to war.'

Chang looked sleepily at his partner and waited till he had finished venting.

'It didn't happen. Meghan dropped her weapon the moment our cruisers showed up. She did it to put the fear of God in them. Beth wasn't even at the scene.'

'Don't you encourage them.' Pizaka shook a warning finger. 'They behave as if they own the NYPD.'

'In a way, we do, Zak,' Beth replied snarkily. 'Know who's good friends with the commissioner?'

Pizaka glowered at her, his lips tight. He didn't need reminding. Zeb and Broker were tight with the NYPD Commissioner.

'What were you trying to achieve?' he bit out.

'Putting them in their place. They're Cole Patten's men.'

'Cole Patten? As in the billionaire?' Chang's eyes widened. 'They said they were security people from some firm.'

'Yeah, but employed by Cole Patten.'

She broke it down rapidly for the cops, and for a few moments, there was astonished silence in the room.

'He really has no proof of his identity?' Chang asked, amazed.

'Well, he's got the standard stuff. Driver's license. Passport. Social Security number. But nothing like DNA or fingerprints to say he's Cole Patten. No birth records. No blood records. Nada.'

Chang wandered out of the room almost lazily, and when he returned fifteen minutes later, he was clutching a sheet of paper.

'No arrest record for him. Nothing for his brother, father,

or any member of the family. There was one incident, when a few neighbors complained about noise levels at his home. Some kind of party. But that's the only record we have of him. He's clean.'

'He has a good lawyer.' Beth snatched the sheet from him and read it swiftly.

'That makes a difference,' he agreed.

'Did he approach the NYPD with this allegation?'

Chang and Pizaka looked at each other and shrugged. 'Not us. We don't exist for him. Want me to check if he went to the commissioner?'

He drew out his cell and turned away before she could reply.

'Wendy,' he spoke softly, 'I need to speak to the boss.'

'It's about Cole Patten. Yeah, him.'

He held the phone to his ear and straightened instinctively when the commissioner came on the line. His voice dropped even further as he asked his question.

He turned around when his call had ended. 'Patten did speak to the commissioner. About a different matter, however.'

'You know who the Russian is? The one who made the accusation?' He paused theatrically.

Meghan sighed. 'Tell us, Chang, before we beat it out of you.'

'Gorbunov. Valentine Gorbunov.'

'Yeah.' He grinned slowly at their expressions. 'The same guy who's supposed to head the Russian mafia.'

# Chapter 6

Gorbunov had an imposing build. He was close to six feet four, with wide shoulders, black hair that fell to his shoulders, and a craggy face.

His hook nose curved over lips that were twisted in a permanent sneer.

A long time ago, his face had been scarred in a knife attack. He bore the scar proudly on his left cheek, not attempting to remove it with surgery.

He was in his sixties, but looked fifteen years younger. A rigorous regimen of diet and hard work kept flab away from his body.

His black eyes glittered as he listened, his phone held close to his ear, and played with a paperweight.

'Buy some more,' he grunted when the caller had finished.

'You heard me.' His voice rose when the caller protested. 'The price will fall some more today. Don't. Question. Me. I. Know,' he roared and crashed the phone into its cradle.

'*Yuri*,' he bawled.

The door to his plush Central Park office opened, and his assistant hustled in.

'Release a press statement. The man who calls himself Cole Patten is an impostor. He is a fraud. All business contracts with him are void.'

Yuri moistened his lips nervously. 'We can't say all that, boss, not in a newspaper. They'll sue us for libel.'

Gorbunov's brows came together. 'We already accused them. This isn't new,' he thundered.

'We informed their board and their lawyers. Going to a newspaper, that's making it public. They'll—'

'Bah. You think I'm scared of their court cases? These Americans. They run to their courts at the first sign of trouble. Patten will know how a Russian fights. We don't go to courts. Do it.' He snapped his fingers and Yuri scurried out.

A man in a dark suit entered the office just as Yuri left.

Daniel Lavrov was Gorbunov's most trusted man. A lawyer by profession, he was the Russian's chief advisor and had been with him ever since Gorbunov had started out in Russia, as a street thug.

'You told him?'

'*Da*.' Gorbunov crossed his elegantly shod feet on the desk and watched his friend peer out the window.

The apartment overlooked the west side of the park and was one of the most coveted units in the city.

Several buyers had been bidding for it when it had come on the market. Gorbunov had doubled the asking price and, after acquiring it, had invited national newspapers and media companies for a party.

He'd been making a statement. Valentine Gorbunov had arrived in America.

Soon after the apartment's acquisition, he'd formed Salaluga Corporation in America, the vehicle for his investments, and started buying mining companies in the US.

And then, he had set his sights on Cole Patten and Chisholm Corporation.

'Not even two years. We have come far, Valentine,' Lavrov mused as he sipped at the black tea a flunky had brought.

'Yes, *brat*. America is not very different from our home country, though,' Gorbunov laughed. 'They called us mafia there. They call us the same here.'

'You have to be careful with that side of the business, Valentine.'

'We have been careful all our lives.'

Lavrov looked up at a slight sound.

A lean man rose from a couch in a far corner of the office. He had been lying so still that neither Yuri nor Lavrov had noticed him.

Novel Kirilov was Gorbunov's hatchet man. His killer. He was the liaison between Gorbunov and the entire army of street soldiers that made up the Russian's gang.

The Russian mafia didn't have one gang or one boss. Like the Italian mafia in the US, it was made up of several gangs.

However, Gorbunov's gang was the most prominent, and *Russian mafia* had become synonymous with Valentine Gorbunov.

The gang's activities ran wide and deep, from bootlegging in Siberia, to contract killing in Moscow.

Like most modern criminal outfits, Gorbunov's had diversified into legal businesses. He owned factories in Russia, oil companies, gas stations, restaurants, and chains of convenience stores.

It helped that his gang controlled the unions in the businesses he owned. A win-win for him.

Gorbunov had visited America several times, and after each visit, his desire to live in that country had grown.

His gang had already had operations in the region. Not just in America, but in Mexico, Canada, and South America.

Once the business with Chisholm Corporation, had gone south just over a couple of years back, he had been determined to move to America.

It had been relatively easy to secure the paperwork and the visas. He, Gorbunov, had never been arrested in Russia. Despite the rumors of his mafia association, or that he himself had killed several men, not one witness or Russian police officer had challenged him.

Gorbunov had connections. He had money, and his story was that he, a Russian billionaire, aimed to invest in America.

He found that the lubricants of money and connections worked in America too. Once he had settled in the new country, Kirilov and Lavrov had brought over his best men. Fifteen of them. All killers, but not ordinary hitters. These were intelligent men, who could blend into the new country, could speak the local language fluently, and didn't look out of place.

Appearances mattered in America.

The killers reported to Kirilov alone. They didn't interfere in the existing criminal operations. They were running smoothly, and there was no reason to change the status quo.

Gorbunov pushed back in his swivel chair and clasped his hands behind his head as Kirilov approached.

His ace killer was lean, pale, his skin tight around his cheekbones. His eyes were flat and never showed any emotion. His dark hair was cut short, and while he was dressed neatly in a suit, appearances didn't matter to him.

Gorbunov had seen him effortlessly toss a portly man over the roof of a high-rise. The victim had been late in protection payments and had pleaded for time.

Kirilov didn't negotiate. If he appeared at a scene, death had arrived. Usually in a painful form.

'He went to a Columbus Avenue building,' the killer spoke softly. He never raised his voice, not even in anger.

'Who's there?'

'Some security consulting firm. Networks. People. Offices. Hostage negotiation. That kind of work.'

Gorbunov stopped rocking in his chair. 'Why would Patten go there?'

'There are two women in that office. Twins. They have a reputation. Good investigators.'

'Like private detectives?'

'*Da*.'

'He's hired them to check out his identity. Maybe investigate us as well.'

'*Da*. That seems likely.' Kirilov brought out his phone and showed several photographs to Gorbunov.

The Petersens from various interviews. In their SUV.

'Who's this?' Gorbunov pointed to one picture of a black man and a blond man.

'Two employees. Ex-Army.'

'They're involved?'

'Don't know. I will get some equipment in their offices.'

Equipment meant surveillance devices. Kirilov wasn't a conversationalist. He used words differently.

'You'll be careful?'

The killer didn't answer. He returned to his couch and went back to his passive state.

'Cole Patten won't know what hit him,' Gorbunov gloated to Lavrov.

'Once his share price tanks, after today's press release, he will come running to me. And then he'll find out what I really want.'

# Chapter 7

Cole Patten was at his desk the next day when Ken Farrell came into his office.

'How're you holding up?'

'Like a punch-drunk boxer.' Patten grimaced.

Ever since Salaluga Corporation's press release, he had been taking calls. From business associates and investors. From the few friends he had, and most importantly, from his board. His board demanded answers and a swift and satisfactory closure to the scandal.

'We might have to act,' his chairman had told him ominously. 'Otherwise…'

Patten knew what that action would be. He would be stripped of his title, his shareholding taken away. Criminal proceedings would follow.

Farrell picked up the remote on Patten's desk and turned off the wall-mounted TV that was on mute.

The media had gone into a feeding frenzy since the story had caught everyone's attention.

Talk show hosts filled their programs with 'experts' who passed judgment on Patten and Chisholm.

The scrutiny took its toll on the company's share price. It was at an all-time low, perfectly priced for Salaluga to snap it up.

'Can't we do anything? Go on the offensive?' the CEO asked his lawyer.

'We've already shot off cease-and-desist letters to the Russians. Threatened to sue them.'

'Posturing?'

'Yes.' Farrell dropped into a chair opposite his client. 'That's all we've got. I have more bad news.'

'What?'

'We no longer represent the company. Your chairman called me early in the morning. Said it would be a conflict of interest. Followed it with a letter.'

He drew it out of his breast pocket and slid it across the desk.

Cole Patten didn't pick it up. A haunted look appeared on his face.

'What options do I have?'

'Prove who you are,' Farrell replied grimly.

'I'm waiting for the Petersens to get back to me.' He raised his hands helplessly.

'They aren't the only investigators in the whole country. For Christ's sake, Cole—'

The door burst open and Beth and Meghan Petersen strode in.

Farrell jumped. 'How did you get in? Cole, call security. They can't barge in here.'

'Down.' Meghan pointed with a finger and drilled the billionaire with a cold stare. 'There's history between you and Gorbunov. What's it?'

Sighing, Cole Patten rose and closed the door. He crossed his arms and leaned against a bookshelf.

'Valentine Gorbunov was my father's partner.'

'Keep talking,' Meghan replied curtly without missing a beat.

'Ken knows the backstory better. I heard it from him.'

'What do you know of Valentine Gorbunov?' Farrell said, taking his cue, replacing his angry expression with a lawyerly one—bland, and patronizing.

*What I wouldn't give to sock him in the chin and wipe away that condescending look...*

Meghan hoped her thoughts didn't show on her face. 'Why don't you tell us?' she challenged him.

'Gorbunov grew up in Salaluga.' Farrell adjusted his cufflinks and flicked a speck of lint from his lapel. 'A town a hundred miles east of Moscow. A mining town, once. Then the mines disappeared, and what remained was high unemployment, and bands of thugs. Gorbunov belonged to one such gang. He joined it when he was very young. Pickpocketing, assault, robbery, those were his occupations. Of course, none of this is proven, you know. There was an unauthorized biography of him a few years back. I'm quoting from it.'

Meghan made a discreet hand sign to her sister when Beth fidgeted.

*Let him speak.*

They had let Werner loose on the Russian and had studied the thick dossier the supercomputer had produced before coming to Patten's office. The lawyer wasn't telling them anything new.

*Let him have his moment.*

'The petty crimes graduated to more serious ones. He's

rumored to have had his first kill at the age of eleven. When he was thirteen, he met one Eldar Sokolov. Sokolov was a member of the Communist Party's Youth Wing. Sokolov was eighteen then. The two became close friends, the criminal and this youth worker. Sokolov became Gorbunov's mentor. Got him to move away from crime. Encouraged him to get into business. Approved of the young Gorbunov getting into steel and automobile factories. The two grew up, and you know what happened to Sokolov.'

'He's the Russian president. And Gorbunov didn't quit crime. He became more sophisticated,' Beth replied drily.

'Gorbunov and Billy Patten. How did they meet?' Meghan asked the lawyer.

'You asked where Billy Patten got the funds from. To buy the mine.'

'And Patten said it was from his mother's family.'

'That's right. What he didn't tell you was that when he was scouting the mines, he met another investor.'

'Gorbunov?'

'Yeah. The young Russian met the war-weary Billy Patten in Chisholm. Before Gorbunov moved to the USA for good. Both he and Billy Patten were interested in the same mine. They liked each other, to the extent that they struck a deal. They would become partners. Pool their funds and buy the mine and operate it together.'

'I thought you said he had no money then.'

'He didn't.' Farrell gave a wintry smile. 'But he was no fool. He had taken a loan out on his house. Used that to make a deposit on the mine. That gave him right of first refusal. He would lose that deposit if he didn't make good on the purchase. And he would lose the house too. However, he didn't tell Gorbunov all this. He gave the impression he was sufficiently funded. The two shook hands over their agreement. The Russian went back to his country to dispatch his share of the funds, while Billy formed Chisholm Corporation, the holding company, to acquire the mine.'

'And then Billy Patten got the investment from Rachel's family, and Gorbunov was no longer required.'

'That's right, ma'am. The Russian felt he had been betrayed. There were heated phone calls and at least one angry meeting that I know of, but the ship had sailed.'

'Why now?' Beth shook her head unconsciously. 'Something doesn't feel right. Why's Gorbunov going all-out now? After all these years?'

'There's something else—'

'That you didn't tell us?' she snarled and whirled on the CEO. 'Patten, if you want us to help you, you and your flunky better come clean. About everything.'

'You can't talk to us like that.' Farrell stood up angrily, his face turning red. 'We have been polite with you, but the two of you are acting like prima donnas.'

'Are you done?' Beth's eyes could have frozen the Sahara.

Farrell clamped his lips tight and darted a glance at Patten. The CEO looked unsettled and out of his depth. He motioned for his lawyer to sit down and turned to the sisters.

'*You* came to us.' Beth's hand jabbed the air like a fencing sword. 'You want us to help you, you tell us everything. Every little detail about what exactly happened.'

'I met Gorbunov, just over a couple of years back.' Patten ran a hand through his hair wearily. Gone was the façade of a man in control. He looked hunted and desperate. 'In D.C., at a conference. He introduced himself. Suggested we merge our companies. I would stay on as CEO. The combined group would be the largest steel business in the world.

'I laughed it off. Didn't take him seriously. He didn't take it well. He brought up the gentleman's agreement with Dad. How my father had betrayed him. I knew none of it, at that point in time, and told him so. Even if I had, nothing would have changed.

'I didn't hear from him until he made that formal offer to my board. We declined it, and he then went hostile.'

'Doesn't answer my question,' Beth rapped out. 'Why now, after all these years?'

'China,' Meghan surmised, recollecting the dossier Werner had put together on Chisholm and Patten. 'You made your first acquisition in China, one of the largest steel plants there. The Chinese government made a big deal about it. They gave you the red-carpet treatment.'

'Yes.' Patten smiled faintly, recovering his poise. 'Chinese steel is everywhere. Chinese companies are on an acquisition spree. We went out and bought this company, and it changed our fortunes. We were now able to ship steel at a lower price than before. We were able to compete with the Chinese on their terms.'

'Your share price rocketed up. You became the hottest steel company on the planet, and that got Gorbunov's attention,' she concluded.

'Yes.' He paused and asked hesitantly, 'You will help me?'

'Yeah.' She didn't need to look in her sister's direction for confirmation. They could sense what the other was thinking. 'We will. The same conditions apply. You don't hide anything.'

'Deal.' Patten shook hands with them, his face lightening.

'What swung you?' Farrell asked them.

Meghan gave him a wicked smile. 'We don't like Russian gangsters.'

She rose, Beth joining her, and prepared to leave.

At the door, she turned back and fired a last volley at Patten and Farrell.

'Just so we're clear, we don't care about Chisholm. We are interested in finding out who *you* are.'

# Chapter 8

The sisters had taken only a few steps to the mirror-polished elevator doors when Meghan caught Beth's sleeve and halted her.

'You notice something? Those dudes were missing.'

'The heavies? Yeah. I didn't see them either.'

They turned back and, for the second time in the day, flung Patten's door open unceremoniously.

The two men started and turned in their direction.

'Your goons—where are they? You know what they did?'

Farrell took a step forward and then stopped on seeing Meghan's set face. 'We heard of it, ma'am. You didn't have to…'

His voice trailed off when she raised her hand to silence him.

'You talk too much, Farrell. I guess you get paid by the word. I wasn't talking to you.'

She looked beyond the lawyer at Patten. 'Why were they following us?'

He looked away in embarrassment. 'I wanted to know what you would do. That could help me influence you.'

'Where are they now?'

'I fired them.'

'Because we spotted them. If they were that good, we shouldn't have noticed them, right?'

His silence was her answer.

'We'll break the legs of the next heavy who follows us.'

Beth winked at her when she slammed the door shut, and they returned to the elevator.

Their vehicle was in the basement parking garage, a cavernous space that held several other vehicles.

It was empty of people, however, and their steps echoed as they went swiftly to the SUV.

Meghan was fishing for the keys, and Beth was circling to the passenger side, when two shadows emerged from behind another SUV.

Meghan whirled instantly and flung her bag away when she recognized them.

The heavies.

'*Beth*,' she warned her sister.

'You don't make us look like fools,' the one in the front growled as he advanced threateningly.

'Back off. You'll get hurt,' she ordered, force and authority in her voice, as her sister joined her.

The two of them crabbed sideways until they were no longer backed up against their vehicle.

Open space behind them. The thugs in front. Menace in the air.

'You heard what she said, Joe? *We'll* get hurt,' the heavy scoffed.

'I'm shaking,' Joe chuckled and rushed at the sisters.

Meghan stepped wide of her twin.

*Joe is Beth's. I'll deal with the other.*

Her attacker came fast, his fist swinging, his eyes narrowed and mean.

She ducked under the blow. The next moment, she was sprawling when a hard left sank into her belly and knocked her sideways.

Her assailant laughed. 'Didn't expect that, did you, honey?'

*Honey. No one calls me that.*

She rolled and got to her feet swiftly, wincing slightly at the blow. He had hit hard, but beneath her jacket and her tee was an armored vest that felt like fabric. It had cushioned most of the impact.

*You got overconfident and paid the price for it*, she berated herself.

The assailant had followed her and was readying for another assault.

She glanced to her left. Beth had Joe in an armlock and was forcing him to the ground.

She kept her eyes on her sister for an extra moment and swiveled only when she felt the rush of wind. Her attacker had charged, seeing that she was distracted.

*My turn for a fake move.*

She met the incoming right fist with her left forearm. Deflected it. Went inside her assailant's stance, her body turning sideways.

She dropped to a crouch, her left leg shooting out to brace herself, and rammed her right shoulder into the man's midriff.

The man's breath left in a whoosh, his guard dropping momentarily. Meghan's right arm flowed up smoothly, turning inward, and her elbow smashed his nose.

His gasp turned into a hoarse cry, and then became a scream when her left palm crashed into his throat. She grabbed him by the left arm and heaved him over her hips, down to the hard floor, bringing a knee to his chest.

'We went easy on you this time,' she panted. 'If we ever see you again…'

She stepped back, not finishing her words, and assessed him. The heavy was beyond causing her any more trouble. He was curled on the concrete, his knees to his chest, moaning softly.

Joe wasn't in any better shape. He had split lips and bleeding cheeks, and from the way he was favoring a side, a broken rib. Or two.

Meghan bent over her attacker and searched him swiftly. She relieved him of his gun, and when she straightened, Beth had taken away Joe's weapon.

They removed the magazines and tossed the guns deep inside the garage before going back to their vehicle.

'You okay?' she asked her sister as she nosed the vehicle out of the garage.

'Yeah. He was less trouble than yours. How about you?'

In response, Meghan parked the vehicle in an empty space on the street, closed her eyes and breathed deeply several times.

The blackness that was threatening to engulf her receded, the nausea abating.

'He hit me hard,' she admitted. 'Never been struck like that.'

She winced when her sister raised her tee and inspected her stomach.

The bruise had reddened and was turning dark. She sucked in a breath when Beth touched it lightly.

'No ribs seem to be broken.' Her sister felt her sides. 'Let's get that checked, in any case.'

Meghan would live, their doctor pronounced drolly. Her clinic was a block away from their office, and she was used to wounded Agency operatives coming in.

'Try not to walk into concrete walls,' she said slyly as the sisters walked out under the night sky.

'We should tell Patten,' Beth suggested as they stood outside and watched the city flow by.

'Nope. If he fired those men, then their attack had nothing to do with him. If he was lying, then let him squirm, wondering how we'll react.'

'And how do we react?'

'We find out which twin died. And go through anyone who tries to stop us.'

# Chapter 9

On TV shows, clues were easy to find. A trail was quickly put together, and by the time the commercials got out of the way, the case was neatly solved.

In Beth and Meghan's world, an investigation took longer and was a lot less glamourous than Hollywood portrayed it to be.

They made a timeline of events the next day.

Billy Patten had married Rachel in 1960. He had gone to Vietnam in 1966, returned after a year, and then went back for another tour late 1967. He came back for good in 1969. He'd bought his mine in Chisholm in 1970. The Patten twins were born two years later, and in 1979, he'd taken them back to Vietnam, where the accident happened.

They stared at the whiteboard on which Beth had written the dates. Nothing leaped out at them.

They turned to Werner and spent the better part of the morning writing algos.

The algorithms were complex programs that searched, or made linkages between disparate events, people, objects—anything that the sisters wanted them to do.

The programs started looking into Chisholm's board, Farrell and his law firm, Patten's friends and his current girl-friend, Valentine Gorbunov and his associates. The sisters cast their net wide and let the supercomputer get on with the job.

They turned their attention to the list of family and friends that Farrell had provided. Dividing the names between them, they hit the phones.

By the time they broke for lunch, no progress had been made.

Every person they had spoken to said the same.

That they assumed Cole Patten was who he was. Nope, most of them said, they didn't remember the brothers when they were younger. The few who did claimed it was hard to distinguish between the two. And that was a long time ago.

What was intriguing was that no detailed financial records existed from back when Billy Patten had been alive.

There were audited financial statements, but that was all that existed.

No bank statements. No ledgers. Nothing.

There was a record of the first steel mine's purchase. Five million dollars changing hands.

There were entries of the steel and hotel businesses going into trust after the Vietnam vet's death. There were records after that, but none before.

Ken Farrell had no answers either.

'I inherited this law firm. It was well run, legally run, audited thoroughly,' he insisted when Meghan asked.

'Wouldn't your father have kept records? Your firm was the company's law firm, after all. Those records couldn't have disappeared just like that.'

'Nothing disappeared.' His voice rose. 'What I know of

Billy Patten is that he kept his financial transactions separate. We didn't handle all that.'

'Who did?'

'He did.'

'Billy Patten handled his finances, his accounting, himself?'

'Yeah. There was an external accountant who did the audits, but they weren't involved in the running of the business. Billy Patten did all that.'

'Where's that accountancy firm?'

Farrell mentioned a name. 'They went out of business. A long time ago. His bank, a community bank, has folded too. Trust me, I looked into that. No one exists from that period. There's no illegal money trail.'

'No one to confirm if it exists,' she replied pointedly.

He hung up.

The sisters went to their favorite hangout, two blocks from their office.

They were alert, keeping an eye on their six, wearing the special shades that Broker had designed.

Those goggles had tiny rearview cameras in the stems that projected in a corner of the lenses. Perfect for discreet countersurveillance.

There was no threat. It wasn't just the heavies the sisters were watching out for, however.

That time when they had been grabbed and taken to Syria, it was on a street like this one that they had been snatched.

They had learned from that incident. Vigilance became part of their DNA.

'We widen the search. Speak to people in Chisholm,' Meghan mumbled over a mouthful of food as they discussed the case and its peculiarities.

'We have to take Farrell at his word. That there was no financial impropriety.'

They had checked out Farrell and his firm. It had a good reputation, and the lawyer himself was well known for his honesty and fair dealing.

'We don't like lawyers, but that's a different matter. Farrell's not the focus of our investigation. Let's concentrate on the boys.'

'We should check with their school. The local PD, hospitals, anyone in authority who might have had contact with the Pattens.'

'Even a few people stepping forward to say Cole is Cole will be good,' Farrell had claimed, in another call with him.

'Why didn't you reach out to anyone?' Beth had asked him.

'We didn't take Gorbunov's claims seriously,' Farrell had replied. 'And by the time we did, the damage had been done. No one wants to get in the way of billionaires' feuds. The rest of the world doesn't really care what happens to Cole or Chisholm Corporation. Besides, we suspect Gorbunov has threatened any witnesses.'

'You sure about that?'

'If I was, I would be filing lawsuits.'

'If there's no one to step forward,' Beth said, toying with her food, 'then there's nothing to be proven.'

'Prove what?' Roger dropped into a chair next to her, Bwana occupying one near Meghan.

Beth eyed them suspiciously. 'You two are tailing us?'

'Not me. I have better things to do. I was sleeping in the office. My looks—the more rest I get, the better they become,' he replied grandly.

Bwana raised his hands defensively. 'Don't look at me like that. I was in the office too. You saw me. Both of us were.'

'And you didn't follow us?'

'Why would we do that?' Bwana asked, all innocence.

'Oh, maybe because you thought we needed following. Protect us from the evils in the world.'

'Nope.' Roger tucked into his meal. 'That's not us. R&R in between missions. That's what our doctor ordered. We aren't shadowing you up and down as you save billionaires.'

'If we find you—'

'We get it. You'll heap all kinds of trouble on us. We aren't shadowing you,' Roger replied solemnly.

If either of the sisters had glanced under the table, they would have seen him cross his fingers.

'What proof were you talking about?' Bwana asked them.

'Cole Patten. If there's nothing and no one…' Beth broke off and stared at her sister, who had a faraway look on her face.

'What?'

Meghan didn't answer.

'Meg.' Beth pricked her hand with her fork. 'What's up?'

'Bwana and Roger,' Meghan replied.

'Yeah, what about them? They're right here.'

'They served together.'

'So? Where are you going with this?'

'They served together,' Meghan repeated again, rising.

'Of course.' Beth caught on quickly and rose too. 'Billy

Patten was a Tunnel Rat. The men he served with—that's a different bond. He'd have been closer to them than to anyone else. He'd have told them anything. Those men could have met the young twins. They would know.'

Bwana looked at their departing backs, mystified, and turned to his friend. 'You know what they were talking about?'

'About me,' Roger replied confidently. 'It's my looks. Women can't help talking about me.'

'Fifth Infantry Division, Mechanized,' Beth read out from Billy Patten's dossier. 'He held the rank of sergeant when he left the Army and returned to the US.'

She brought up a photograph on her screen and zoomed in on it for her sister to see.

Billy Patten was a short man, about five and a half feet in height. He was smiling in the picture as he was descending into a hole in the ground, a handgun in his right hand, a flashlight in the other.

He was bare-chested, and on his chest, there seemed to be the faint marking of an old wound.

Beth scrolled through more photographs that Werner had dredged up from various archives and personal email accounts. The supercomputer went where the sisters asked it to, hacked into the accounts that they ordered.

There weren't that many images, however, and Meghan sent a message to Cole Patten to send more photographs, if he had any.

'There's a blog here somewhere. I came across it when I was researching Patten,' Beth muttered under her breath as her fingers danced over keys. 'There!'

The blog was by the son of another vet, who was

chronicling the lives of Tunnel Rats. He had extensively interviewed several veterans, one of whom was one Leroy Duhan.

'Billy Patten was the one of the first to volunteer,' Duhan had told the blogger. 'He didn't know any fear. You should remember, the tunnels were new to us. We had never experienced combat like that. That didn't deter Billy. He signed up right away. He was the first of the Tunnel Rats.'

Beth looked away from the screen to her sister, her eyes shining. 'We should talk to Duhan.'

It turned out that Duhan was from the Fifth Infantry too and had served in the same unit as Billy. Him and eight other men.

Ken Farrell emailed a black-and-white photograph of Patten with his buddies. It had been taken in Vietnam two years before his return to the US.

Ten men, looking straight at the camera, some of them in their uniforms, the others more casually dressed. Patten was resting his hands on two men on either side of him. One of them was Duhan; the other was one Pete Garrett.

Billy, Duhan, and Garrett were to the left in the picture. Beth read out the other names from Cole Patten's email as Meghan wrote their last names on top of each person. Bartley, Ezell, Munoz, Deering, Bielecki, Wolfgram, Paschall, and Vollmer.

'Those two.' Meghan pointed at the men on either side of Billy. 'Let's talk to them first.'

That turned out to be easier said than done. The ten men were from the same unit but came from different states. Neither Farrell nor Patten had any idea where the men were, or if they were alive.

'Where are his belongings? He must have kept his letters, ribbons, his personal effects, somewhere.'

'In Chisholm,' Cole Patten replied. 'In the family home. It's locked up. We left it there once I moved to New York. I've hardly been there.'

'You haven't gone through whatever's in that house?'

'No. Farrell's people went through it, catalogued everything. They would have told me if there was anything important. There wasn't.'

*Billionaires*, Meghan shook her head. She scrawled a reminder to herself—*Visit Chisholm*. However, a lot could be done without leaving the city.

The sisters resorted to old-fashioned detective work.

Meghan looked up records of death, while Beth called the Department of Veterans Affairs.

There were several deceased Duhans and Garretts, but after an hour's search, Meghan found out that none of them were the men they were seeking.

*That's good. These records aren't comprehensive, but hopefully they're still alive.*

She turned to Beth, who seemed to have run into a bureaucratic wall.

*Call Clare*, Meghan mouthed at her.

Beth nodded, spoke briefly, and hung up.

She called Clare and put the phone on speaker.

Their boss listened without interruption for a while, while Beth outlined the case and the information they were seeking.

'I'll get those details to you. Shouldn't take long,' she replied when Beth had finished. 'Sounds like an interesting case.'

'Yes, ma'am. That's why we took it on.'

'Billy Patten. That name rings a bell. Hold up a moment.' She returned after a moment. 'Found it. The FBI and the IRS were interested in him for some time. Source of funds for the first acquisition. It got cleared up. They said he got an investment from his wife's family?'

'Yes, ma'am.'

'That's correct. The case was closed.'

'The IRS was satisfied, ma'am?'

'Yes. Beth, Meghan?'

They could hear a smile in her voice.

'Yes, ma'am?'

'Try not to kill Gorbunov. We're watching him. He's of more value to us alive than dead.'

'We'll do our best, ma'am.'

They met the Russian sooner than they expected.

He came for them.

# Chapter 10

They had stepped out for a break in the evening when a limo drove up in front of them.

Three suits moved towards them, all smartly dressed, moving with the same liquid ease that their friends had.

A fourth man came around the vehicle.

Meghan shoved Beth away, started reaching inside her jacket, when Fourth held his hand up.

'No harm.' His voice was guttural, thick.

*Feels like a Russian accent.* Meghan looked around swiftly. There was no one nearby, just the four men.

*I can take two of them, Beth the rest. If it comes to shooting.*

'We want you to meet someone.' Fourth was calm, unconcerned by the Glock that showed beneath her jacket.

'Who?' Meghan asked warily.

She was looking for signs of a trap but couldn't spot any. The remaining suits were relaxed, their legs spread wide, hands empty, dark shades on their faces, all looking in the twins' direction.

All four men were in grey suits, polished black shoes, confident in themselves.

*These aren't like Patten's heavies. These dudes are way better.*

'Valentine Gorbunov,' Fourth replied. 'We will bring you back. Alive.' There was the barest smile on his lips.

'We aren't bothered about that,' Beth snarked. 'You need to think about whether we'll leave *you* alive.'

The smile left Fourth's face. He moved to the limo, opened its door and gestured stiffly at them.

Meghan followed Beth, pressing the button on her left cuff as she climbed inside.

Her cuff buttons were alarms that linked to Werner. The supercomputer in turn broadcast the message to the operatives who were around.

The left button was for *Something weird happening*, while the right one was for *In trouble. Come shooting.*

All the suits clambered in the front, which made her wonder how large the vehicle was.

*Large enough to accommodate all of us, for sure.*

The inside was soft leather in muted colors. More than sufficient leg room. Arm and headrests. A console in each of the armrests.

Beth squeaked in delight when she pressed a button and a built-in massager came to life.

'There are drinks in the bar in front of you,' a disembodied voice came through the speakers.

'Why don't you just drive?' Beth snapped back, then closed her eyes and went back to being massaged.

'Why do you think he wants to meet us?' she asked Meghan.

'To check us out.'

The four suits escorted the sisters inside a marble-walled and pillared building. It had an enormous lobby, a large chandelier hanging from the high ceiling, and discreet security.

Fourth took the lead and guided them to a bank of elevators.

He spoke softly into a mic in the wall panel, and the doors opened.

The car was large enough to hold twenty people and was done in carpet, gold leaf, and brass mirrors.

It didn't have any buttons to be pressed, no floor lights.

It opened into a large hallway, a burly man standing guard.

He ran a detector over them and silently held out two trays. They placed their Glocks in them and, when he didn't move, put their cell phones in the containers.

'Jackets.' He pointed.

They removed those too.

He ran another detector over their bodies and finally nodded at Fourth, who led them inside an enormous room.

At one end was a walnut desk, a few chairs around it, and at the other end were several couches.

Fourth took them to the desk and bade them seat themselves.

Meghan swiftly checked out the room. No sign of Gorbunov. The four men lined up behind them. Large shaded windows to their right, through which Central Park could be seen.

There was no sound in the room. Insulation kept out the street noise and deadened any interior sounds.

A man coughed, clothing rustled, but other than that, there was only silence.

That broke when a hidden door to the side of the desk opened.

Valentine Gorbunov emerged, followed by a man in

an expensive-looking brown suit, both of them talking in hushed whispers.

Gorbunov stopped on seeing the sisters and frowned.

His brow cleared as he clicked his fingers as if just remembering.

'You are the babes helping Patten.' He smiled widely, displaying even, white teeth.

Russian mafia heads could afford dentists, good ones at that.

*Babes.*

Meghan looked at Beth and the two rose silently and started walking out of the room.

The four heavies blocked them, staring back impassively.

'What? You don't like my company?' Gorbunov growled, then laughed. 'Babes? You didn't like that? I am sorry. Come, come. Please sit. I am sorry. You see, I am new to your language. In Russia, for me every woman is babe.'

Beth raised her eyebrow at her sister, who nodded imperceptibly.

They returned to their seats and watched as Gorbunov made a show of rolling back his sleeve, glancing at an expensive watch and mumbling under his breath. Brown Suit stood silently, watching, observing, his face impassive.

'You are wondering why I wanted to meet you?' he asked when he was done with his routine.

'Nope,' Meghan replied. 'You wanted to see how good we are.'

The Russian scowled, and then his face cleared and the smile returned. 'You are smart. Good. That makes it easy for me. We don't need to go into history. I am sure you know it.'

The warmth disappeared as quickly as it had arrived. 'Stop

helping him. You work in a security firm, no? Go back to your jobs. Don't get in the way of Patten and me.'

'Why?'

'Because I asked. Nicely.' A feral look appeared on his face. 'In my country, when I ask nicely, people do it. Otherwise they see my not-so-nice side.'

'You are in our country, however.'

'Your country, my country. It's the same. Same jungle. More fancy cars and big buildings here, that's all.'

'Why did it take so long for you to wake up? You met his father years back. But you approached Cole Patten only recently. Why?' Beth asked, curious.

They had their own routine. Meghan went in hard and aggressive, Beth played sweet and nice. They didn't hesitate to use their looks and feminine charm, if needed.

'I was growing.' Gorbunov flung his hands out expansively. 'Sokolov was a star, and I was helping him. Billy Patten's rejection hurt. Bitterly. I lost big opportunity. But I put my ambition on hold. Sokolov was more important. Now he's big, I am also big. It was time to make contact again.'

'You are a businessman. I'm sure you have lost deals before. Why is this so important? Is it because of China?'

'China? That's important to Salaluga Corporation. My honor is important to me. Billy Patten dishonored me. Then his son did the same. Nobody does that to Valentine Gorbunov.'

'Nobody knows and nobody really cares what happened.'

'I do,' he said fiercely.

'You have a big ego.'

'*Da.* Huge. Bigger than Russia or America, or the two combined.'

'You intend to kill Cole Patten?'

'No,' Gorbunov rasped. 'He has to live to see what crossing me means. He won't die. But he won't live happily ever after.'

'He may not be Cole Patten. Your allegation might be right.'

'Don't care. Salaluga will buy Chisholm, and I will crush Billy Patten's son, whoever he is.'

'You talk big for a thug,' Meghan said contemptuously. 'You're just a parasite. You rode on Sokolov's coattails in your country, and now you're trying to act as if you're big and important. You aren't.

'I'm glad you sent your limo,' she continued without letting him respond. 'It saved us a ride. We were going to call on you. To tell you that we have no great interest in knowing who Patten is. His is an interesting problem, but we took on that case because of you. We love taking Russian gangsters down.'

She paused for breath. Gorbunov didn't speak. His face was flushed. His big hands opened and closed, but he didn't utter a word.

'You won't crush Patten, because we will destroy you before that.'

Valentine Gorbunov snapped.

# Chapter 11

He yelled inarticulately and surged across the walnut desk.

Meghan heard commotion behind her. The suits moving. Someone yelling, Beth's chair squeaking.

She paid no attention to any of it.

Gorbunov's face filled her vision. His eyes were mean, and he was mouthing curses as he lunged over the vast desk, his hands reaching out for her.

She reached forward instead of evading.

Slapping his groping palms away, she grabbed him by the collar and smashed the side of his head on the desk.

She rammed her elbow into his temple, applied pressure, and only then looked up.

The four suits had their guns out and had closed in on Beth and her.

'*Stop!*' Brown Suit was yelling.

'Release him or we shoot,' Fourth hissed.

'Back off,' Meghan countered calmly. 'If I apply enough pressure, I can severely damage him.'

'We will shoot,' Fourth shouted.

'Go ahead.'

'*Stop!*' Brown Suit roared, silencing everyone. 'Ma'am, please let him go. Grigor, you and your men stand down. Both Valentine and the visitors have said their piece. This stops right here.'

Meghan snatched a glance at him and caught the faintest look of pleading on his face.

She relented and moved away.

'No, Valentine. Don't say a word,' Brown Suit warned in Russian when the mafia boss rose, spitting mad.

Gorbunov didn't say anything. His eyes filled with hate as he glared at the sisters. He gave a sharp nod to Grigor. 'Take them away.'

The heavy sheathed his gun, his men following suit. They crowded the sisters and herded them to the door.

'That was a bad move, babe,' Gorbunov called out as they reached the door. 'Now you have me as an enemy, and I am the worst one anyone could wish for.'

'Is that the best you've got, Gorbunov?' Meghan chuckled. 'You should do your research better. You don't know us. Now, you will.'

Gorbunov straightened when they had left his office. He wiped his mouth and looked at the palm. There was a smear of red on it. He dabbed his lips with a paper towel and threw it carelessly aside.

'Are you okay?' Lavrov asked, concerned.

'Yes. This is just blood. There will come a time when I shed theirs.' A slow smile spread across his face. 'I am a good actor, no?'

Lavrov relaxed in return. '*Da*. You think they bought it?'

'Of course,' Gorbunov sniggered. 'Any thought they had

of stopping, cutting Patten loose—gone. They will be more determined now to find out.'

'You are sure there's something to be found?

'*Da.*' The mafia boss exuded confidence. 'I know Billy Patten didn't have enough money, even after the family loan. That mine cost five million. The rest of it came from somewhere. We are talking about millions.'

Lavrov rubbed his jaw reflexively. 'He could have been lying to you.'

Gorbunov went to the large windows and watched in silence, his hands on his hips.

'No,' he said softly. 'He wasn't. We told each other everything. I told him about my kills. He told me about his, in Vietnam. He said he had been involved in a racket there. Something illegal. Didn't go into many details. We bonded, like men do who have the same ambition. It was only when that other money came that he changed. He was my friend until that point. Then he betrayed me.'

'You can investigate yourself. You don't need the Petersens to find this for you.'

'We have covered this,' Gorbunov replied in irritation. 'You are the one who advised me to keep a low profile. The FBI will be watching me. Maybe other agencies. It is best this way.'

He stared at a couple of female joggers moodily. They looked like the twins, and as they ran in the park, their blonde hair bounced up and down their necks.

He had visited America one last time before his permanent move to the new country. He had gone to Chisholm, to inspect other mines for acquisition.

There, he had met a former employee of Billy Patten.

That man, Jim Rogish, had somehow slipped through the security cordon around the Russian and said he knew Gorbunov.

'Saw you that last time, when Billy and you came to Chisholm. I was in the diner, behind you guys. Overheard your plans.'

'So?' Gorbunov replied, bored.

'I was his foreman. I worked in the mine he bought. Ran a tight ship for him. And then he canned me.'

'Get to it.' Gorbunov was distracted. Such tales didn't interest him.

'He betrayed you.'

'Don't I know it?' he scoffed.

'He lied when he said he got the money from his wife's family. They only lent him a small amount—three million. The rest of it came from outside. Outside the country.'

That caught the Russian's attention. He withdrew a roll of bills and peeled a few off.

'Tell me everything.'

Rogish didn't have much more to tell. Late one night, Billy Patten had been drunk in the mine.

He had come to the foreman's office and leaned against the door. 'They think I'm a hero.' He weaved and straightened. 'What do they know?'

'You've done well, boss. Built a steel business up from nothing. That's something to be proud of.'

'And you know who helped me?'

'Your wife's family?'

'They did, some. But a lot of it came from outside.'

'Outside, boss?'

'Yeah. From another country. You're a good man, Jim. Stay like that.' And with that, Patten had walked away.

'I tried to find out,' Rogish said quietly. 'I asked discreetly. Patten came to hear about my investigation and he fired me. On the spot.'

Gorbunov pursed his lips, wondering if there was anything in Rogish's story. He paid the foreman and returned to Russia.

The story had remained at the back of his mind. He relocated to America, had tried to investigate himself, but Lavrov had dissuaded him.

'You don't understand,' Gorbunov had protested. 'If Billy Patten had illegal funds, that interests me. Where did the money come from? And is there more of it? It will also ruin Chisholm, if it's true. I can buy it for nothing.'

'Don't.' Lavrov had been curt. 'You have a reputation. There will be eyes on you. Stick to clean business.'

And then he had heard of the twins, and everything had fallen into place. The twins would find everything about Billy Patten. He wouldn't need to lift a finger. All he needed to do was keep tabs on them. He had good people for that.

And if there was nothing about Billy's funding, nothing illegal, then Gorbunov wouldn't have wasted any resources.

All he had needed to do was give the sisters a nudge. Make them more motivated.

After studying their files, he knew the only way to do that was by antagonizing them.

Gorbunov was pleased with his day's work when he left the office.

Lavrov was with him, as was Grigor.

He took the elevator to the ground floor, making small talk.

He strode out, confident, sure of himself, a Russian mafia head who had nothing to fear.

And then he saw the two men leaning against his car.

# Chapter 12

'That him?' Roger chewed a toothpick as Gorbunov and his men came closer.

'Let's see.' Bwana crossed his arms. 'Looks like a thug, walks like a thug, is accompanied by thugs. Yeah, that's him.'

Grigor stepped around his boss, his hand waving imperiously. 'Step away, please. That's a private car.'

'We know that, dude. Why do you think we parked our butts here?' Bwana laughed. 'We want to talk to Gorbunov.'

'No talking.' Lavrov closed in. 'We don't know you. Make an appointment if you want to speak to Mr. Gorbunov.'

'Now *that.*' Roger grinned. 'You bring up an important point. We don't want to speak to him. Not really. We don't even like him. He's an insect. But we have to talk to him.'

Lavrov stopped, Gorbunov behind him, Grigor to one side. 'What's this about? Should I call security?' He turned his head and addressed the security man in Russian. 'Grigor, where are your men?'

'Those suits? Three of them?' Bwana asked him helpfully in the same language. 'They're in the car. Indisposed. Stomach problem. Grigor, you really need to recruit better men.

They just fell down when we went near them.'

'What do you want?' Gorbunov barked.

'He speaks,' Roger exclaimed, though there was no humor in his eyes. 'I think that was meant for us.'

'Seeing as there's no one else here, I would assume so.'

'I don't have time for this,' Gorbunov said through clenched teeth. 'You have five minutes, and then I am calling the police.'

'Beth and Meghan Petersen. Stay away from them. Don't send cars. Don't talk to them. No contact. We see any of your goons near them, they won't walk away. Not on their own two feet.'

'You are threatening my client,' Lavrov snapped even as Grigor surged forward, his hand reaching under his jacket.

Bwana jabbed him in the chest before the heavy's gun appeared. Grigor lost his balance and stumbled. Before he could recover, Bwana put his hand around his shoulder.

Only a close observer would notice it was an armlock that restrained the Russian.

'Yeah, that's a threat. What are you going to do about it?' Roger spat out his toothpick insolently.

He let the tense silence build for a moment before he nodded at his friend.

'Don't choke Grigor. Boss man has to yell at him. He has to stay conscious for that.'

Bwana released the heavy, and the two sauntered away, disappearing into the pedestrian traffic.

'Who were they?' Gorbunov choked out, his face red in rage.

'They work in the same firm as the sisters.' Kirilov appeared beside him, as if conjured from thin air. 'Bwana and

Roger. Bwana's the black man. Should I take care of them?'

'No.' The anger receded from the mafia boss's face. 'We need the sisters. They'll do our work for us.'

Zeb slurped his juice noisily as he stared curiously. That's what tourists did.

He had a camera around his neck, a map by his side, a backpack on his shoulders, and a Yankees cap on his head. Tourist attire.

He was in a juice bar opposite Gorbunov's building. He had a good view and had watched the byplay, inwardly amused.

*Bwana and Rog. Only they could pull off a stunt like that.*

Zeb had followed the cab driver outside the Columbus Avenue office and had tracked him to Gorbunov's office. He had then researched the Russian and read up on the backstory between him and Billy Patten.

He made a louder slurp when Kirilov appeared.

*That dude's new. He wasn't in any of the files*. He snapped several photographs discreetly and watched the killer.

*No wasteful movements. Eyes constantly moving. I bet this guy's good. Very good at being bad.*

He sent the pictures to Werner as the pale man spoke to Gorbunov briefly and went back inside the building.

Zeb decided to hang around.

*He has to emerge sooner or later. Then I'll follow him.*

Beth and Meghan, unaware of all that had happened, were on their phones.

Clare had come through and had sent them the addresses of the nine other men in Billy Patten's unit.

Three of them, Bartlet, Munoz, and Bielecki, were no more. They had died some years back.

Duhan and Garrett were still alive. Garrett was living in Nice, France, while Duhan was in Granbury, Texas.

Beth snapped her fingers, signaling for her sister to stay quiet.

'*Oui*, ma'am, Pete Garrett,' she said in French.

*He's living with his daughter-in-law*, she whispered to her sister.

'*Non*, ma'am. He doesn't know me. I would like to talk to him. About one of his friends. Billy Patten.

'*Oui*, ma'am. I will wait.

'Mr. Garrett.' She switched to English and straightened. 'I'm Beth Petersen, sir. I wanted to talk to you about Billy Patten. I don't know if you've been following the news in America, sir.'

She broke it down for him quickly and waited for him to digest it.

'No, sir. We haven't spoken to his wife's family. Only distant relatives are around.

'We, sir? That's my sister, Meg, and me. We take on interesting cases, sir.

'No, sir. We aren't a detective agency. We work for a security consulting firm. We advise the NYPD on cases. I can get the NYPD commissioner to give you a call, sir, if that helps. Yes, sir. I can do that. Sure, sir. I'll call you back.'

She made a face when she hung up. 'He wants a reference. I said the commissioner would call him and confirm we are who we say we are.'

'So what are you waiting for?' Meghan urged her. 'Pick the phone up. Call Commissioner Rolando.'

Bruce Rolando, the NYPD commissioner, had a soft spot for them. He was friends with Zeb and Broker. He had met the sisters during one case the Agency had helped on, and had been deeply impressed by their ability to connect the dots.

He had a standing offer for them. They could join the NYPD as special consultants whenever they wished.

Beth dialed his number and spoke to his executive assistant.

'Sir, I come seeking a favor,' she told him when he came on the line.

She spoke quickly and then smiled when she hung up.

'He'll do it. He says we're wasting our lives working with the old people in this office. You located Duhan?'

'Yeah. He's in a nursing home. Let's see where we get with Garrett, and then we'll turn to him.'

Pete Garrett didn't turn out to be very helpful. He spoke freely once the commissioner had called him, and he seemed to be impressed by the sisters' connections.

However, he didn't have much to say about Cole and Josh Patten.

'Billy shared their pictures,' he explained. 'But, you have to remember, ma'am. This was the 1960s, and we were in 'Nam. We didn't carry a whole load of photographs with us. Those boys, they looked so alike in the pictures Billy shared, it was hard to tell them apart.'

Beth nodded unconsciously. Strangers found it very hard to tell Meg and her apart, they looked that similar.

'You never visited him, sir?'

'Just twice, ma'am.' Garrett continued to address them despite Beth's request. 'Once, we had a shindig, after we all returned. This was in a hotel in Chisholm. Lot of people around. I spent time with my unit. I'm afraid I don't remember much of anyone's family.

'The second time was another gathering, five years after we returned. Like an anniversary. Same bunch of people. My memory is just as bad.' He gave an embarrassed laugh.

'Did Billy Patten tell you anything about his family?'

'A lot. That boy couldn't stop talking about his kids. But nothing that would help you identify them.' He broke off, thinking, and then resumed, 'No, ma'am. Can't recollect anything. We stayed in touch when we returned, but by then, his life had changed drastically. He'd become a businessman. He spoke about his business, his travels, his 'Nam trip, that kind of stuff.'

'You met him just the two times after returning, sir?'

'Yes, ma'am. Leroy was closer to him. Much closer. You speak to him?'

'Not yet.'

'Try. You might get somewhere.'

Leroy Duhan was in a nursing home in Fredericksburg, Texas. From her first call, Meghan got a sinking feeling.

*This isn't going to go well.*

The receptionist at the home was a battle-axe who protected the residents' privacy fiercely.

She neither confirmed nor denied Duhan's presence.

'I don't care if you're the president, or the pope,' she snapped when Meghan cajoled. 'I don't give out such information.

''What if I was Elvis?'

'That might work. Can you sing? No? Didn't think so.' She hung up.

Meghan looked up and grinned ruefully at her sister's expression.

'You think she might tell me if I dressed in sequins and carried a guitar?'

She picked the phone again without waiting for an answer.

'Ma'am,' she pleaded with the receptionist, 'this is important. It concerns Leroy's friend, Billy Patten. They both served in Vietnam.'

'Honey, you know this is a nursing home, don'tcha?'

'Yes, ma'am.'

'You know what kind?'

Meghan blinked. 'No, ma'am.'

'It's for those who are dying. Those who are in bad shape. Mr. Duhan, if he was here, which I can't confirm or deny, wouldn't be in a position to come to a phone. Not in this home.'

Meghan smacked her forehead with her palm.

'We'll come there, ma'am.'

# Chapter 13

The sisters set off to JFK, where the Gulfstream was waiting.

Meghan didn't notice the other black SUV following them at a distance. Even if she had, she wouldn't have made out Bwana and Roger in it.

Neither of the operatives spotted the yellow cab tailing them.

Zeb did. He was shadowing the cab, the same one that had been parked outside their office.

'Fredericksburg is small. About ten thousand people. Founded in the 1840s. German settlers,' Beth read out as the aircraft took off.

'What about the nursing home?'

'She was right. It provides care to those who are in the last stages of a terminal illness.'

'How come we missed that about Duhan?' Meghan groused as she worked on her screen, reading the vet's file. 'It's not in here.'

'People who are dying don't advertise it,' her sister replied sarcastically.

Beth closed her screen and pushed her seat back.

She wriggled her toes in the plush leather and glanced at her sister, who raised an admonishing finger.

'Don't!'

Beth pouted but kept quiet. She never failed to comment on the luxurious seats whenever they flew in their aircraft.

'They're heaven,' she burst out after a while and warded off the cushion her sister flung at her.

An SUV was waiting for them at San Antonio airport.

They had similar vehicles cached in garages in big cities all across the nation, and in several other countries too.

The garages were owned and maintained by veterans who provided the vehicles as and when the operatives needed them, took them back after a mission, and kept them ready for the next.

Each garage was paid for from a fund that Zeb and Broker had created for former military personnel.

Meghan drove swiftly, and when she eased into an empty parking space at the nursing home, it was hot and dry outside.

*Normal for Texas.*

She donned her shades and paused for a moment to get her bearings.

The home was on South Washington Street, a compound wall separating it from the bustle of traffic. The building was red brick and was surrounded by a lush garden and several leafy trees.

It was an oasis of calm, and when they walked up the driveway, several of the residents were relaxing on benches or in their wheelchairs in the garden.

Meghan pushed open the double doors and waited while the sole receptionist behind the desk dealt with other visitors.

She recognized her immediately from her voice. She was in her fifties and had frizzy, white hair, granny glasses, and a string of pearls around her neck.

She joked and laughed with residents and had a permanent smile on her face.

She aimed that towards the sisters as Meghan approached her.

'I'm Elvis,' Meghan introduced herself.

She didn't react for a moment and then burst into a guffaw.

She came around the desk and smothered the twins in hugs and went back to her chair.

'I still can't tell you if Mr. Duhan is here.'

'It's like this, Debbie.' Meghan read her name plate and made a spur-of-the-moment decision to confide in her.

Trust won the day.

Debbie listened without interruption and then rose from behind the desk.

She beckoned to a coworker and asked her to man the desk.

She then led the sisters through winding hallways and past several rooms.

*Bright colors. Cheerful. Residents seem to be well-cared for.*

'What's he suffering from?'

Debbie stopped and shook her head sadly. 'He suffered from PTSD when he returned. Didn't get treatment in time for that. Then a liver problem went undiagnosed for a long time. Turned into cancer. Failing organs. Fading memory. Honey, that man fought for us, and now he's fighting his last battle.

'You may not get your answers,' she warned as she knocked on the last door in the hallway. 'He goes in and out, and even when he's aware, he can mix realities.

'Leroy,' she called out. 'You have visitors.'

Leroy Duhan was frail-looking, his shirt and trousers hanging limply on his skinny frame. He had thinning hair and watery eyes. His hands shook as he fumbled with the TV remote and turned the volume down.

He turned towards the sisters and looked at them blankly for a moment before smiling.

'Visitors. Don't have many of them.' His voice was strong as he pointed to a couple of chairs.

'Mr. Duhan, I'm Meghan Petersen, this is my sister Beth. We've come from New York, sir.'

'New York. Fine city. Visited a few times.'

He lapsed into silence as he squinted at them. 'Do I know you?'

'No, sir. We're working on something. We're investigators, sir, working on a case. Someone you know. Do you remember Billy Patten, sir?'

'Billy.' He clapped softly. 'Of course, I know him. Fine boy. He did well. He's alive?'

'No, sir,' she replied gently. 'Billy died several years back, in Vietnam.'

'No, no. He came out alive. With me. We survived.'

'Sir, he had gone back.' She eased into the backstory, taking her time, making him comfortable, and when she had finished, he sat in silence.

'I remember now. I spoke to him a few weeks after he had come back. He said he was planning to take his kids to Cu Chi.

'I liked Billy.' He wiped his eyes. 'He was different. Not

like us. He liked to cut corners. That was why he was so good in the tunnels.'

'Cut corners. Like what, Mr. Duhan?'

'Brenda. She was good to me. I loved her.' He started weeping silently.

In confusion, Meghan looked at Debbie, who made a calming gesture with her hand.

'His wife. He lost her soon after he returned. They never had children. He'll be back. This is how he is.'

Duhan got back to full awareness half an hour later and reminisced about his friend. He didn't talk much about his time in Vietnam, except to say all of them were lucky to be alive.

He spoke about Billy Patten's business. 'He told me about some Russian, and then the next day he calls me and says Rachel's family helped him.

'"What about the Russian?" I bellow down the line.'

'"Oh, him. I'll just say sorry." That was Billy. He could be your best friend, but he could also cut you loose. Just like that.'

He fell silent, gazing at a photograph on a wall. Duhan, surrounded by his unit, the same picture that Farrell had sent them.

'He had a dark side. Not many knew of it. I think even Rachel didn't know of it. Once he told me it wasn't just her family who helped him.'

'Who were the others, sir?'

He shook his head. With Beth's help, he rose slowly and went to the picture. He ran his fingers on it lightly and returned to his chair.

'I didn't ask, ma'am. It wasn't something I wished to get involved in.'

*Ask him about the sons*, Beth whispered to her sister. *Before he fades.*

'His sons, sir?' Meghan bobbed her head at her twin. 'You met them?'

'Several times,' he chuckled. 'I used to visit them every year when Brenda died. Right until he took them to Vietnam.'

'You could identify them, sir? Many people seem to be unable.'

'Me?' he scoffed. 'Yeah. They looked like mirror images, but I had a simple solution. If I was confused, I used to ask them to strip.'

'Strip, sir?' Meghan asked, confused.

'Yeah. Get them to remove their shirts.'

'Why, sir?'

'There was that mark.' He looked at them in surprise, as if everyone knew about it.

'What mark, sir?'

'Josh had a scar on his chest. Above the right nipple. From an accident when he was very young. It never faded.'

# Chapter 14

'We can't believe what he said. Not without further confirmation.' Beth toyed with a lock of her hair as Meghan drove them back to the airport.

They had spent a further hour with Duhan and had left when he'd started to tire.

The vet had told them a lot, not all of it useful to their case, but he had started flagging the more he spoke.

'He contradicted himself a few times. The first time he said the scar was on Josh. The second time, it was on Cole,' Meghan agreed.

Debbie had called time when she saw Duhan slipping in and out of reality. 'That's the most time anyone has spent with him.' She thanked them. 'He hardly gets any visitors. His face lights up when he has some.

'You get what you wanted?' She gave them a searching look.

'Not quite.' Meghan mentioned the scar, and the receptionist nodded in understanding.

'Yeah, that happens a lot. He's a good man, however. If he remembers anything more and tells me, I'll call you.'

'What now?' Beth demanded when they were back in the aircraft.

'We go to Chisholm. Visit the family house and search through whatever's there. I'm surprised there aren't any photographs of the brothers—in fact, of the entire family. The ones Farrell and Patten sent aren't very helpful.'

The images the billionaire and his lawyer had sent were studio photographs. The four members of the Patten family, formally dressed, staring intently at the camera. Various poses, either in a group, or individually. There were a lot more pictures of Billy Patten in Vietnam than of the young children or any other family member.

'Neither Billy nor Rachel believed in photographs,' had been Farrell's explanation when Beth had pressed him.

'Yeah.' Beth brought them up on her screen and scrolled through them rapidly. 'No birthday parties. No picnic photographs. Nothing. Are we going to tell them about Duhan's revelation?'

'We have to.' Meghan fished out her cell.

The outcome of the call wasn't what she or Beth expected.

Farrell immediately arranged for a press conference and broke the news that a witness would prove Salaluga's accusations to be wrong. 'We have conclusive proof that the CEO of Chisholm Corporation *is* Cole Patten. We have an independent witness, Leroy Duhan, a vet who served alongside Billy Patten.'

'You can't do that,' Meghan yelled at the speakerphone in their vehicle as she drove back from JFK to their office. 'Leroy Duhan is the last person you should drag into his. His awareness and memory aren't what they used to be. He's dying, for Chrissakes. We can find some other way to prove Patten's identity.'

'You know what the share price is today? My job is to do what's best for my client. Cole Patten has no scar on his chest. That's proof.' He hung up.

She swore a blue streak, rolling down her window and giving the finger to a cab driver who honked angrily as he overtook them.

By the time they reached their office, there was a further update.

News channels reported that Cole Patten was flying to Fredericksburg, along with his lawyers, to get a recorded statement from Leroy Duhan.

The media went to town with the story. One war hero coming to the rescue of a fellow soldier. What's more, the two had served in the same unit and were fast friends. Black-and-white pictures from Vietnam rolled on screens across the country.

This was the stuff that won awards and shot ratings to the roof.

The twins watched in dismay as talking heads came on the air, heads nodded, tongues wagged and predictions were made.

Chisholm's share price registered an uptick.

They went to their apartments, which were on an upper floor, to shower, and when they returned, there was another development.

Daniel Lavrov, Gorbunov's lawyer, had given an interview, discrediting Duhan's comments.

'He's old. We know he doesn't have full possession of his faculties. In any case, we too will be flying to Fredericksburg. We'll take our own statement from Mr. Duhan. We are sure the CEO of Chisholm *isn't* Cole Patten,' he said scornfully to a bunch of reporters, paraphrasing Farrell's line.

Beth rose silently from the couch, turned off the TV and strode to the elevator.

'We should be in Fredericksburg, too.'

The town was a changed place when they arrived four hours later. Neither the Chisholm nor the Salaluga party had arrived yet.

From snatches of conversation, they gleaned that both were expected in the next hour.

South Washington Street was crammed with TV vans, police cruisers, and throngs of spectators.

People bunched in front of the nursing home, many of them recording on their cell phones. Reporters thrust their mics in front of random townspeople and asked them about Duhan.

One intrepid newsman approached Meghan as the sisters shoved through the crowd towards the home.

'Ma'am, do you know Leroy Duhan?'

The next moment he fell back, his nose bleeding.

'I'm sorry,' Meghan gushed sweetly. 'Someone jostled me.' She shoved him away and raced to the entrance.

She pushed the door open, Beth crowding behind her, and froze.

Debbie faced them, her hands on her hips. Gone was the smiling woman who had welcomed them.

'Get out,' the receptionist hissed.

'Debbie, this wasn't our—'

'*Out!* John.' She waved imperiously at a security guard. 'Make sure these two don't enter the building.'

'We can't blame her, sis.' Beth patted Meghan's hand.

They were in a café on Main Street, watching a wall-mounted TV along with fifty other customers in the room.

They had slunk away, unable to meet the receptionist's eyes.

The restaurant provided a refuge as they watched the events unfold.

Farrell and Patten drove up in an SUV with tinted windows, cops clearing a path for it. Reporters surrounded the vehicle when it rolled to a stop, but neither of the men answered any questions. They ducked from the cameras, ran to the nursing home and disappeared inside.

Daniel Lavrov came fifteen minutes later. He stepped out, buttoned his jacket, smiled a lot, and answered a few questions.

He stood at the door, turned and waved at the crowed, and went inside.

'I want to wring his scrawny neck,' Beth muttered, drawing a weak smile from her sister.

Forty-five minutes later, Farrell and Patten emerged. They were tight-lipped, their faces pale, and they didn't take any questions.

'No comment,' were the only words that escaped the lawyer's lips as he escorted his client to the waiting vehicle.

'That's not a good sign,' Beth whispered and zipped up when Meghan shushed her.

Lavrov appeared thereafter, a triumphant look on his face.

He addressed the reporters like a general who had won a war.

'Like we suspected, Mr. Duhan's testimony wasn't conclusive. I can't say anything more, except this. We still believe the man posing as Cole Patten is a fake. An impostor. We will prove that in time.'

The crowd exploded. Questions were hurled at him. Cameras flashed. People surged forward.

Lavrov milked it, dishing out high-wattage smiles until he too left in his vehicle.

The nursing home's director was the last person to come out. He made a brief statement accusing both parties of causing distress to Leroy Duhan. Of sucking the vet into their petty fights.

'Mr. Duhan has served this country well. He is a hero. He is dying. He suffers from PTSD.' The crowd fell silent.

'We told both parties that interviewing him was pointless. He frequently gets his facts wrong. He should be left in peace. However, each party bulldozed their way in before we could stop them. You have seen the results. I would like the town of Fredericksburg and all visitors to leave us alone. To let us do our job—which is caring for our heroes.'

Beth felt small, and when she snuck a glance at her twin, she knew Meghan felt the same.

They had set out to prove Cole Patten's identity. All they had succeeded in doing was shredding a war hero's dignity.

# Chapter 15

They didn't quit, and neither did they give up. They returned to New York that night and made a call to Cole Patten.

Farrell answered.

'We don't want to speak to you,' Beth told him.

'I'm sorry,' the lawyer told them awkwardly. 'I mishandled that one. I should have heeded your advice.'

*Maybe he's not that bad*, Meghan mused as Beth stared at the speakerphone.

'Where's Mr. Patten?'

'He's right here.'

'You don't have any scars on your chest?' she asked when the CEO came online.

'No, ma'am. If what Duhan told you originally was right, I am Cole Patten.'

'Doesn't mean anything now. Not after what your fancy lawyer pulled off. I bet your stock has plummeted some more. Maybe your board has called you to whisper some sweet nothings in your ear,' Beth said derisively.

Patten's silence was his reply.

'Your Chisholm home—any caretakers there?'

'Yes. You're going there?'

*What do you think, dumbass?* Beth nearly spat out, but she restrained herself when her sister placed a calming hand on her shoulder.

'Yes. Neither you nor Farrell went through your family's belongings, did you?'

'Not to any great extent, ma'am. Ken sent some people, but they returned with no proof.'

'Tell the caretakers we're coming. Any of your mom's relatives still there?'

'An aunt. Maybe more, I don't know. They aren't of much help—'

'We'll decide that,' she cut him off and hung up.

'Dumbasses,' she snarled at the phone, smiling reluctantly when her sister laughed.

'Go to bed,' Meghan urged her. 'We'll fly out early in the morning.'

'And if we don't find anything there?'

'Let's cross that bridge when we get to it.' The elder twin waved dismissively.

Meghan sat alone in the office once Beth left, watching the city lights through the darkened windows. They were thick and had all sorts of proofing on them. Only a rocket or a tank round would get through them.

*What would Zeb do?*

She turned it over in her mind, tempted for a moment to message the operative and seek his advice.

*Nope. He's in Syria. In a war zone. He'll have enough on his plate.*

Zeb had changed their lives. Before they'd met him, they

were running their web and design agency in Boston. They were doing well. Good clients. Steady growth. But they both knew something was lacking.

They came from a cop family in Jackson, Wyoming. Their father had been a highly decorated officer who had lost his life in the line of duty.

The sisters always received a warm welcome whenever they returned to their hometown.

They had met Zeb in Wyoming while on a vacation. That holiday had turned into a nightmare when a gang of assassins had pursued them for no apparent reason.

A lean brown-haired man had come to their rescue. Zeb. They had discovered much later who he really was, and from then on, had discovered purpose in their lives.

Doing something that was bigger than running a business. Serving their country. Helping the vulnerable.

They had badgered Zeb to let them join him. He had refused. They had then gone after Broker and had gotten him to make a case for them. Zeb had then caved in.

They'd sold their business in Boston and relocated to New York, and they hadn't looked back.

*This is our town now. New York. This is where we belong.*

Along the way, Beth had found love. *Not me.*

Meghan knew she wasn't cut out for the kids-and-white-picket-fence lifestyle. The Agency. Zeb. The rest of the operatives. Beth. They were her universe.

A light rain started, became heavy and diffused the streetlights, blurring the outside world.

She padded silently to the elevator and left for her apartment.

They flew to Chisholm the next day.

The city was in the center of the Mesabi Range, one of the four large iron ore deposits that made up the Iron Range in Minnesota. The minerals were scattered around Lake Superior and extended into Canada.

The mining towns in the region experienced a boom or bust depending on the vagaries of the national economy and international trade.

Back in the fifties, the mines had supplied steel to Detroit, supported construction jobs and war efforts.

As the world's economies had become more interdependent, imported steel had become cheap, and that had led to the decline of the Iron Range mines.

There were still a few operating mines that transported mineral by rail to Duluth. From there, they were shipped to processing mills in Indiana and Ohio.

Chisholm wasn't a large city. Approximately five thousand people in a five-square-mile area. A mining museum, a lake, Lake Longyear, and a few other attractions.

The sisters flew to Range Regional Airport in Hibbing, where another black SUV was waiting for them.

Their destination was twelve miles away from the airport, and by ten am, they were driving through the quiet streets of the city to West Lake Street, which proceeded towards the lake.

They didn't go to the lake. Meghan hung a right on Second Avenue and crawled to a stop in front of a large red brick house with white pillars.

The residence had several parking spaces in front of it, and a stone driveway that was guarded by imposing metal gates.

She announced herself at the metal box next to the tall

barriers. The gates swung open silently, enabling her to drive inside.

She parked in front of a porch, and they climbed up a few steps.

A uniformed black man rose from behind a desk.

'You're the Petersens?'

'Yes.' She removed her shades and looked around.

The lobby was converted into an office. Doors at the far end presumably led to the inside of the house.

'It's very quiet,' Beth remarked.

Carl, the guard, shrugged. 'It's an empty house, ma'am. Not a museum. No one other than me.'

'You come here every day?'

'I stay in the compound, ma'am. There's a small house behind the main building. That's where I live.'

'Have you been here long?'

'My pappy used to be caretaker. I took over when he passed away. Been a few years now. It suits me. It pays reasonably well. It's quiet. Just what I wanted.

'All the boxes are over there.' He pointed to the doors. 'If you go past the living room, and to the library, you can't miss them.'

They didn't.

The cartons were stacked on the floor, neatly labeled and wrapped.

The library had a handful of shelves, on which were a few books and record albums. It had two round tables and a few chairs arranged around each.

Meghan heaved one carton onto a table. Beth attacked another carton, and they delved into Billy Patten's life.

Their day was interrupted just once, when Meghan's cell rang.

'Are you still in Texas?' Bwana inquired.

'Nah. In Minnesota today. Why?'

'Minnesota? What's there?'

'Checking out Cole Patten's folks. You need something?'

'Rog and I wanted the jet. Never mind.'

'You going somewhere?'

'Florida. There's nothing to occupy us here.'

'We're on a case. Work takes precedence over a vacation. You'll have to fly commercial.'

'Yes, ma'am.'

She hung up and went back to her files. It was later that she realized Bwana could have looked up their location on Werner. He would have known they were in Minnesota.

Each one of them had GPS tags in their clothing and shoes. Their supercomputer tracked them at all times. Except when they were undercover, as Zeb was.

*Bwana*. She shrugged mentally. *He doesn't like Werner.*

'You think they bought it?' Roger asked his friend.

'Yeah.' Bwana stifled a yawn and stretched his legs.

The two of them were in a black van a couple of hundred yards away from the Patten residence.

They were equipped for surveillance. Binos. Listening devices. Thermal imagers. Drones.

They didn't expect any hostile action; however, they were prepared for that too. The rear of the van had enough weapons in it to start a war. Or end one.

The sisters had no luck with any of the cartons. They contained mundane papers. Bills. Letters. Certificates.

Purchase documents for the house. School report cards. Vehicle purchase records.

No photographs. Nothing to shed any light on their case.

Beth rose and stretched several hours later and watched her sister wander down the shelves.

Meghan picked up books randomly and leafed through them.

There were several on Vietnam and mining. She flipped through the pages quickly and put them back.

Beth joined her. Two could go through the library faster.

Afternoon became evening. Shadows lengthened. Outside, a chair creaked.

Beth sensed it first.

Her sister freezing. Going still.

'What?'

Meghan didn't reply. She turned a magazine around for Beth to read.

There was a report on the page about Tunnel Rats. Nothing about Billy Patten or his unit.

Meghan pointed to a scrawl in a margin.

A simple sentence.

*Dang changed my life.*

# Chapter 16

Zeb was hanging around outside Gorbunov's Central Park residence again.

He had followed the tall, pale man the day Bwana and Roger had confronted Gorbunov. However, he had lost the man in traffic.

Werner had run the man's face through all the databases it had access to and had come back empty.

Zeb had then emailed the photographs to his contacts—the heads of several intelligence agencies around the world.

Mossad had been the only outfit that had returned a positive response.

Avichai Levin, the head of the Israeli unit, had sent another photograph to Zeb.

*Kirilov. Former Spetsnaz. Killer. Runs Gorbunov's criminal enterprise. Gets involved in special situations*, Levin wrote.

*Why isn't he in any database?* Zeb asked him.

*No one knows he exists*, came the reply. *Except us. We know everything.*

Zeb knew Levin's boast wasn't far out. Mossad's

intelligence-gathering ability was the envy of many Western agencies.

He studied Mossad's photograph of Kirilov as he waited.

It had been taken in Moscow and showed the killer emerging from a nightclub. Even in the picture, his alertness came through. His flat eyes had been sweeping the street as the camera had clicked.

Levin's dossier had been thin. Kirilov had grown up in the same town as Gorbunov, in Salaluga. He too had been an orphan.

No one knew how the two had met. However, if there was one man Gorbunov trusted, it was the killer.

*He has no nicknames*, Levin had warned him.

Zeb knew what that meant.

The most lethal men didn't need alternate names.

Zeb pulled his cap lower over his head as Kirilov came out of the building.

Zeb was on the other side of the street, a backpack on his shoulder, a map in his hand.

He studied it every few moments as he watched the Russian linger on the pavement for a few seconds.

Kirilov went to the nearest subway. Zeb followed, paralleling him.

The killer didn't go underground. He continued walking, seemingly lost in thought, and reached the West Sixty-Sixth Street entrance to Central Park.

He looked back once and then entered the oasis of green.

Zeb hung back.

The park had less traffic. The Russian would make him.

*I can wait outside.*

In Chisholm, the twins compared the line in the magazine to several of Billy Patten's letters.

That scrawl was his.

They took photographs and sent them to Farrell and Cole Patten, along with a question.

*Who is Dang?*

They checked into a hotel near the lake, and the next day, they went to visit Ginny Davis.

Davis lived in a small house on Eighth Avenue Northwest, in Chisholm.

A four-bedroom house with a neatly maintained front yard. A truck in the driveway, no sounds of pets, as they approached her door.

Meghan rapped the knocker, and presently, an elderly woman opened the door.

She had a small hunch, thinning white hair, and wrinkles on her face, and she used a cane.

'No donations,' she told them firmly. 'I give to the church each month. I have no more to give.'

'Ma'am, we aren't here for that.'

She pushed her glasses back on her nose and came closer to them.

'I don't know you.'

'No, ma'am.'

'I don't talk to strangers.' She started to close the door.

'Ma'am, we're here about Billy Patten.'

The door stopped moving.

'Him?' she exclaimed in disgust, but she opened the door wider.

*No love there.* Meghan smiled as she and Beth followed Davis inside.

'Who are you? Why are you asking about him?'

'We're from New York, ma'am. I don't know if you follow the news.' Beth took the lead and gestured at the silent TV in a corner. 'Those accusations about Cole Patten's identity. We're looking into those.'

'Why?'

'He hired us, ma'am.'

'You're detectives?'

'No, ma'am. But—'

'Private investigators?'

'Not exact—'

'What are you exactly?'

Beth waited before responding, to see if she would interrupt again.

Ginny Davis didn't. Her eyes were bright behind her spectacles, her hands steady as they clutched her cane. She sat upright in the quiet home, but for the hum of a fridge from somewhere inside.

'We're consultants to the NYPD, ma'am.' Beth reached out and presented her card to Davis.

She glanced at it once and placed it on a table beside her.

'I watch TV. Follow the news. I know what's happening. How does this concern me?'

'Can you identify him?'

'No. Saw the boys just a couple of times, when they were very young. I wasn't close to them.'

'You are his aunt, ma'am? Rachel Patten's sister?'

'Yes. Her elder sister. Our folks had just the two of us.'

'And you weren't close to her?'

'Nope. Not after her marriage. Billy Patten kept us apart. He had no time for us. Except when he needed our money.

And there were my views.

'I have no interest in helping Cole Patten. Or whoever he is,' she declared before either sister could question her last comment.

'Neither do we, ma'am.'

Ginny Davis looked at Beth sharply. 'What do you mean?'

'We want to find out who he is. Cole or Josh. We aren't the least bit interested in his company's problems.'

'Why do you care?'

'I too suffer from amnesia, ma'am. I don't remember an entire part of my life.'

Ginny Davis opened up after that. She went into how Rachel Patten had grown increasingly distant from her family.

'I don't know if he had anything to do with it. He was a charmer, and of course, once he returned from Vietnam, there was this hero thing about him. My sister didn't speak much about him. About Billy Patten, the person.'

She served them cookies and made coffee for them as she spoke.

'The few times I met him, he was polite. Gentlemanly.'

'You didn't seem to trust him.' Beth grabbed another cookie and bit into it. Cookies. They made the world go round.

'I didn't. There was something about him.'

'What about your husband? What was his reaction to Billy Patten?'

'I never married, my dear.' She chuckled on seeing their expressions. 'I was the talk of the town. In those days, it was expected that women would find husbands. Have a few children. Keep the home and bring up the kids. I wanted none of it. I taught in the local school. Was a feminist. Went on marches, protests. I didn't like the war. Maybe that was a reason why

Billy and I didn't get along well.'

*That's what she meant by views.* Beth eyed another sweet treat on the plate and pulled her hand back when Meghan gave her an icy look.

'He asked your father for money. How did that happen?'

'He didn't. He sent my sister for it. My folks did well for themselves with Happy Stay.'

'Happy Stay?'

'The hotel chain they had.'

Beth glared at Meghan when her sister made a curious choking sound.

*She's laughing at that cheesy name. That was the sixties, though. Cheesy was in.*

'Dad didn't quibble. He just said he hoped Billy would put it to good use. He didn't expect it back, either. But Billy Patten returned it. With interest.'

'That mine must have been a few million, even in those days?' Beth ventured.

'Five,' Ginny said, confirming what they had discovered in their research.

'Your family lent him all of it?'

'Three. Billy made arrangements for the rest of it.'

'Three?' The sisters leaned forward at the same time.

'Not five?' Beth asked.

'No. Three million. Why do you ask?'

'That mine cost five million, ma'am. Cole Patten and Ken Farrell told us all the money came from the family. If your father lent him only three million, why would they lie?'

'They weren't lying. My dad lent him three. Billy raised two, but routed the balance of that money through my father.'

'Why, ma'am? Why did your father agree? And where did

those other funds come from?'

Ginny shrugged. 'I don't know. He made arrangements. That's what Rachel said. Why Dad agreed, I don't know. He didn't talk business with us.'

'Did your sister say anything about where the two mil came from, ma'am?'

'Nope. We used to talk very casually. She didn't like my stance on the war. She thought it was a betrayal.'

Beth sat back, having exhausted her questions.

'Ma'am, you heard about Leroy Duhan?' Meghan filled the silence.

'Yes.' Ginny's eyes flashed. 'That was your doing? Finding him?'

'Yes, ma'am.'

'You should be ashamed of yourselves.'

'We are, ma'am.'

Ginny brushed aside her apology. 'I didn't support the war. Doesn't mean I had no respect for our soldiers. What those two lawyers did to Leroy was despicable.'

'Yes, ma'am.' Meghan's eyes didn't waver from Ginny's face. She wouldn't make excuses. She wouldn't duck away. She would face whatever was thrown at her.

Ginny Davis stared at both of them, and then her gaze softened. 'I guess you aren't entirely at fault.'

'We are, ma'am. We shouldn't have told Patten's lawyer about him.'

Ginny nodded absently. 'It's done. And no. I don't know of any scar.'

They spent a couple of hours more with Ginny Davis and left with no more information than when they had arrived.

A picture of Billy Patten was emerging. A man who seemed to wear many masks. A war hero for sure, but no one seemed to know who was underneath that.

A man who had raised two million on his own, from sources no one knew of.

They hung around town and went to the location where the community bank had once been. In its place was a convenience store.

The manager didn't know of any bank. He was a recent arrival to the town and didn't have much time for them.

Beth brought up a list of names on her screen. Friends, neighbors, people the Pattens had hung out with.

They went to the residential parts of the city and spent several hours interviewing the people.

Most of those remembered Billy Patten and the twins. None of them could distinguish the two, however.

They drew blank faces when they asked about Patten's source of funds.

'Rachel's family helped him,' was a common refrain.

They trudged to a diner when evening fell. Swirled their straws in their drinks, and it was only then that Meghan remembered.

She brought out her cell and turned the screen towards her sister.

*Dang? Sounds like something dirty. Never heard of it or him. Cole hasn't either.*

'That's from Farrell?' Beth asked.

'Uh-huh.'

'Now what?'

'We set Werner on the money trail.'

'Werner didn't find anything before. In fact, it didn't find the discrepancy. That two mil came from somewhere else.'

'Ginny Davis could be wrong. It was a long time back.'

'You really think so, sis?'

'No.' Meghan sighed and smiled wryly. 'I don't think Ginny Davis could be wrong about anything.'

'Where does that leave us?'

'We go to Cu Chi.'

# Chapter 17

On their return the following day, they briefed Farrell and Patten in the lawyer's midtown office.

'I don't remember Aunt Ginny. I mean, I'm sure I knew her…' The billionaire trailed off.

The takeover and his troubles were showing on him. There were hollows underneath his eyes, and stubble on his chin.

*Didn't stop him from hanging out with that Hollywood actress*, Meghan thought.

The media had camped outside Patten's residence and office. They watched his every move. Every social event he went to was covered.

In contrast, there was no coverage of Salaluga or Gorbunov. There had been just one piece in a newspaper about the Russian's origins and his links to the mafia.

*I guess American billionaire with his back to the wall makes for better ratings.*

They had discussed the mysterious two million at length, but neither Farrell nor Patten had any answers.

It was news to them, and neither had any ready explanation.

'As far as the money and paper trail show, the funds came

from Rachel's father,' Farrell answered stoutly. 'If there was anything illegal about it, it would have come to light by now.'

The sisters didn't let up. They questioned the two men, but inwardly, they knew neither had any answers.

*If Werner couldn't find anything, that means there's nothing to be found*, Meghan transmitted to her sister with her eyes.

There was no connection between the mysterious funds and Cole Patten's identity. They would park the money angle temporarily.

'Dang?' she prompted the men.

Farrell shrugged. 'I went through all the records I have. Correspondence. Got Cole to go through any papers he has. No idea who this is. Or what, if it's a thing.'

'Sounds like an illegal substance,' Patten offered.

'You have any other leads?' Farrell asked them.

'You don't find it suspicious? That there's no record of the two million?' Meghan asked.

'We've been through this before,' the lawyer said exasperatedly. He crossed his feet and jiggled a leg impatiently.

'Maybe Rachel's father had a change of heart. Who knows?'

'And Ginny Davis's statement? You don't find that unusual?'

'That's just one person's account. We are audited. We're a public company, now.' Farrell cast his arms wide in a gesture of helplessness. 'Everything's above board. What do you want us to do?'

'It's hard to believe that a lawyer of your reputation wouldn't look into that two million.'

'Today is the first time I'm hearing of it,' Farrell exploded. 'I went through every sheet of paper, every email, when I took over this firm. Know what I found? Zip. The origin of the funds is clear. Chisholm is clean. My firm is clean. We aren't even representing Chisholm anymore. Conflict of interest, the board said.

'You won't know this, but I told Cole a long while back that if it turned out that any of his dealings were illegal, I would drop him.' He strode to his desk, grabbed a file and riffled through several pages.

He found what he was looking for and thrust it under Meghan's nose.

'There.' He pointed with a perfectly manicured finger.

Meghan read swiftly and passed the file on to her sister. It was a condition, couched in legalese, under which Farrell could sever ties with Patten and Chisholm. It stated that if Patten or anyone from his family, or Chisholm Corporation, had indulged in any illegal activity, Ken Farrell would walk away.

'Satisfied?' he snarled.

'Is your conscience satisfied?' she shot back.

The lawyer snatched the file away and turned his back on them.

'What will you do now?' Cole Patten inquired quietly, in an attempt to soothe his lawyer.

'We're going to where all this started. Vietnam.'

Farrell spun around. 'What do you think is there?'

'We'll know when we find out.'

Meghan called Clare after leaving Farrell's office.

She held up a finger to silence her sister, who was about to burst out in anger.

'Ma'am, it's Meg. We returned from Chisholm yesterday.'

She broke it down rapidly for her boss.

'Yes, ma'am. She said the family lent Billy Patten only three mil. You said the IRS had investigated him?'

*Relax. Take deep breaths. Farrell isn't our enemy*, she whispered to her sister, and got a scowl in return.

'I'm here, ma'am.' She listened intently, then thanked Clare and hung up.

'She says there's a statement by the agents who interviewed Billy Patten. He provided proof that the five mil came from Rachel's dad. They interviewed the father. He confirmed it. End of their investigation.'

'We have only Ginny's word about the three million.' Beth frowned. 'I don't want to believe that she lied to us.'

'She repeated what she was told. Nothing in it for her to lie. Let's see if Werner can sniff anything out. But let's also get to Vietnam.'

Zeb was watching them from a distance, from his tired-looking Toyota. He had spotted Bwana and Roger in their vehicle.

This time, there were no other watchers.

However, he was uneasy. His radar was quiet, but that didn't mean anything.

*If Kirilov can control his chi like I can, I won't sense him.*

He climbed out of his vehicle and followed the sisters as they made their way to a restaurant.

Bwana and Roger rolled to a stop closer to the establishment, but stayed inside their vehicle.

Zeb window-shopped for an hour until the sisters emerged.

He fell in behind them, and then he spotted Kirilov.

The Russian seemed to come from nowhere, walking fast, quicker than those around him.

He was heading towards the sisters.

A hundred yards behind them.

Zeb crossed the street, careful to stay away from the edges of Kirilov's vision.

He fell in behind the killer.

A snatched glance. Bwana climbing out. Purpose on his face. He was fifty yards behind the Russian, Zeb well behind him.

Kirilov didn't look to his left or to his right. He cut the distance down.

Twenty-five yards from the Petersens.

Zeb jogged lightly, wondering what the Russian was up to.

Then Kirilov reached inside his jacket.

Bwana burst into a sprint, as did Zeb.

The sisters were unaware of what was happening behind them. They were conversing intently, their shades on their faces.

Zeb opened his mouth to yell out a warning.

It died on his lips when the killer veered past the twins. His right hand came out. A pair of sunglasses flashed in the light.

He placed them over his eyes, spun on his heels, and caught Zeb's eyes.

He raised his left hand, made the shape of a gun with his fingers, and aimed it at Zeb.

*Got you*, his mocking smile seemed to say, and then he vanished into a crowd of tourists.

'He made us.' Bwana wiped sweat off his face and flicked it off his fingers angrily.

He and Roger knew about Kirilov. Zeb had briefed them.

They hadn't spotted him until then.

'He wanted to draw us out.' Zeb scanned the pavement futilely, knowing the Russian had disappeared. 'He wants us to know that he knows.'

'You didn't detect him?'

Zeb shook his head. 'I spoke to Levin yesterday. He says Kirilov is unlike any other killer we've gone up against.'

*He's as good as you, Zeb. Maybe better*, the Mossad head had warned him.

'He could have killed the sisters.'

'Yeah. Way I figure it, killing isn't on the table. Not yet. He and his boss, Gorbunov, want to know what the sisters are up to.'

'Good.' A wide smile split Bwana's face when Zeb looked quizzically at him. 'Rog and I, we were getting bored. We have a worthy opponent, at last.'

Nothing fazed Bwana. Not even someone like Kirilov. A nuclear weapon could have exploded over him, and he would still be smiling.

Zeb punched him lightly on the shoulder and walked away.

His crew. They were the best.

*Gorbunov can throw whoever he wants at the sisters. Kirilov. Other thugs. Anyone. Not one of them will get to the twins. Not again.*

He was thrown that evening when Roger called him.

'Vietnam?' he asked in disbelief.

'Yeah. That's what Meghan said. They're going to Cu Chi. They want to trace Billy Patten's movements. Talk to people there.'

'They have a starting point? Anyone ready to talk to them?'

'You know Beth and Meg. There aren't many people who will refuse to speak with them.'

Zeb nodded unconsciously. 'You should follow.'

'We were planning to. You coming?'

'Nope. I have a Russian killer to attend to.'

# Chapter 18

*Vietnam, 1967*

'We got to go into the tunnels.' The speaker was tall, a shade over six feet, swarthy, and bare-chested. He smoked a cigar as he addressed the ten men ranged in front of him.

Staff Sergeant Bob Templeman was a legend. He was on his third tour of the country and had the scars to prove it. His right shoulder bore the marks of a badly healed gunshot, when a VC sniper had attacked him.

The skin on his left fingers had whitened. He'd never said why, and rumors abounded.

He never asked his men to do something that he wouldn't do himself.

He was a fierce fighter, a patient leader, and it was no surprise he commanded the loyalty of the ten men facing him.

He hadn't lost a man in his third tour. It was an enviable record, but deep inside, he knew it wouldn't last. Heck, he didn't know if he would leave the country alive.

It was 1967. Templeton and his men were near Saigon. It was the second year since American troops had been committed to the region, to support South Vietnam in their war against North Vietnam.

The war had started as conflicts often did. North Vietnam, a communist state, wished to unify Vietnam by force and went to war with South Vietnam.

The north was backed by the Soviet Union, China, North Korea, and the Khmer Rouge.

South Vietnam had the support of the US, which sought to contain the growth of communism in the region. Australia, New Zealand, the Philippines, South Korea, Taiwan, the Khmer Republic, and the Kingdom of Laos were the south's other allies.

North Vietnam's war was supported by the VC, Viet Cong, in the south. The VC, or Charlie, was the military arm of the National Liberation Front and had the same goal as North Vietnam: unification of the north and south, and the establishment of communism.

The US forces had B-52s, Hueys, Agent Orange, artillery, and tanks. The NVA, North Vietnamese Army, couldn't match the Americans in terms of firepower, but they had numbers. They were close to half a million strong, and the Viet Cong had another three hundred thousand.

The NVA and the VC waged guerilla warfare against their better-equipped opponents.

They hit and ran, hiding in villages.

When the Americans followed them there, in seek-and-destroy missions, they took to the jungles.

The anticommunist forces used napalm and Agent Orange to destroy vegetation.

The communist forces kept on battling their opponents, however.

And the VC? They went underground.

The Vietnamese had started building tunnels in the 1940s, during the French occupation of the country.

That network was built in the Iron Triangle, which was between the Saigon River and the Tinh River. The clay in the region became soft and easily worked during the rainy season, which was when most of the digging was done.

The surface was covered with bamboo and trees of different varieties, making it easy to conceal entrances, create fake ones, or build lethal traps.

During the Vietnam War, the VC repaired the tunnels in the Cu Chi region in the Triangle and developed them into an elaborate architectural marvel.

The cunningly designed underground passages, which ran for hundreds of miles, linked villages and passed below American bases.

The tunnels didn't run straight. They curved; they had hidden doors that led to other tunnels.

There were ammunition stores, ventilation shafts, and even rudimentary hospitals where the injured VC could be operated on.

The Viet Cong even had theaters in several tunnel networks, where propaganda plays were held.

'You heard of the Tunnel Rats?' Templeman angrily drew a puff when none of his men replied.

'I'm waiting.' He cupped his ear theatrically.

'Yeah, Sarge,' Leroy Duhan murmured. 'Who hasn't?'

The Rats went where no ordinary soldier dared. They

climbed down, beneath the ground, and cleared each tunnel of the VC.

The tunnels had been discovered by accident, as the anti-communist forces pursued the VC in the Iron Triangle.

The pursuers, to their frustration, found that their enemies seemed to melt into the jungle, popping up every now and then to fire on them.

They found caches of rice and food as they went deeper in the forest. But not enough VC to justify those food stores.

On the banks of the Saigon, a soldier had sat down to rest on the ground and immediately jumped up when pricked.

He thought he had stumbled into a trap, but when the brush and foliage had been cleared, they'd discovered a concealed wooden door, with a nail for a handle.

The first tunnel had been discovered.

'They've been right below us, all along.' Templeman stabbed his cigar in the air. 'We go hunting them, these dudes vanish into thin air, making us look like fools. All along, the VC were underground, laughing at us.'

Templeman and his men were in the Cu Chi Base Camp, the US military base for several battalions.

'Right below our noses,' he yelled angrily. 'They've been spying on us, shooting at us, and we didn't know. Well, that's gotta change.'

Leroy looked sideways at his close friend Billy Patten and made a face.

It didn't look like the sarge was leading up to any good news.

'We gotta go after them. We need to find them and fight them where they are. We need to go underground.' His neck cords stood out as he screamed.

'We are, aren't we, Sarge? The Rats are taking the fight to them.'

'Not enough of them.' Templeman swiveled and pinned him down with sharp eyes. 'We lose Rats almost every day. We need volunteers. You will make me proud by stepping forward.'

No one came forward.

Templeman's face became an iron mask. He ground his cigar against his fatigues and slipped it into his pocket.

'Not one of you is man enough to be a Rat?'

*No, sir. Not us. We'd like to go home in one piece*, Leroy thought.

He kept silent, however, staring straight ahead when the sergeant walked down the line of soldiers.

'I thought I had fighting men with me,' Templeman roared. 'I seem to have pussies.'

Pete Garrett stepped forward. 'I'll do it, Sarge.' He swallowed nervously.

'*Get back*,' Leroy hissed at him.

'He's right.' Templeman overheard him. 'You're too tall for the tunnels.'

The shorter men in the unit seemed to shrink at that.

A silence fell over the camp. A Huey appeared in the sky, whirling over them for a moment, its blades washing up dust, and then it flew away.

Templeman followed it with his eyes, and when he turned back to his men, he quelled a satisfied smile.

He had his Tunnel Rat.

Billy Patten had stepped forward.

# Chapter 19

'Do you know what you're doing?' Leroy harangued his friend when they were alone.

'No.' Billy smiled wryly as he stripped off his undershirt and toweled himself down. He had returned after a briefing with a few other Rats in the camp.

They had given him several tips on dealing with dangers in the tunnels, and on staying alive.

He would go down the next day, in a section of the forest near the river.

'Do any of us know what we're doing here?' he chuckled.

'Relax.' Billy clasped his friend and grew serious. 'Leroy, you think any of us will get out alive? We have the best-armed soldiers, and yet Charlie's still out there. I've thought this through. If I die down there, I might get a medal. Even if I don't, folks back home, in Chisholm, they'll raise money for Rach.'

Leroy nodded stiffly after a moment. He knew about Billy's history. His friend came from a family that didn't have anything. Just the one house that Billy had inherited from his folks. Billy and Rachel's circumstances hadn't improved after marriage.

His friend had worked in the mines for a few years and had then joined the Army, figuring it to be a better employer and paymaster.

Rachel lived alone in Chisholm while he was away, teaching at the local school. 'Besides, who in our unit could be a Rat except me?' Billy put on clean clothing, then folded the dirty clothes and tucked them in a laundry bag. They washed and dried when they could, when Charlie gave them some respite. 'I'm the shortest in our unit. I knew Sarge had me in mind when he started off on that.'

'Those Rats told you anything useful?' Leroy clapped his friend on his back gruffly.

'Yeah. Get my ass back in one piece.'

'You're a hero, Billy,' Duhan said quietly.

'Nope. I'm just another scared soldier, hoping to get out of this awful place in one piece. Just like you, and Pete, and heck, even Sarge.'

The next day was hot and humid when Billy went to the hole. It was near the river and had been discovered a few days earlier.

It needed to be cleared, a job for Billy Patten, the newest Rat.

Leroy was with him, as were Pete and a few others from his unit.

Templeman stood at a distance and watched with an inscrutable face.

Billy looked at the hole in the ground, taking a deep breath as Leroy fastened a harness beneath his shoulders and fist-bumped him.

He didn't have to say any meaningful words. He, Leroy, and Pete had had the *talk* the previous night. Leroy would sort out matters at home, for Rachel, if Billy didn't return.

'Let's go,' he told his friends.

He climbed down awkwardly, looking beneath him. All he could see was darkness.

'Don't shoot me when I come back up,' he joked feebly, and then the tunnel swallowed him.

Dark. Damp. Stale air—these were Billy's immediate reactions as he hit the bottom of the tunnel, removed the harness and tugged at it.

It slid up silently.

He looked up at the dim light from above, and then crouched, focusing his mind on his task.

The tunnel was small and narrow, suited to the body size of the VC. Billy was similar in height to most Charlie, but he was wider in the shoulders, and they scraped against the walls as he crawled forward.

He had a headlamp that illuminated the immediate few feet ahead of him. He held his .38 in his right hand, sweat streaming down his face as moved forward three or four steps and stopped to listen.

He knew the tunnel he was in was a straight-down tunnel. It went seven feet down and then angled.

The VC sometimes booby-trapped such tunnels with a stick-triggered grenade.

There was no such device in his hole. He had made sure before planting his feet.

Other times, the tunnel could be separated from others by a thin partition.

Charlie could be standing on the other side with a spear, which he would ram into the unsuspecting Rat.

Billy forced the negative thoughts out of his mind.

His goal was to check the hole out and dispose of any VC he found, and then plant an explosive. Once he had climbed out again, they would detonate it and destroy the tunnel.

Billy came to a turn and stopped. He swallowed, breathing shallowly and listening.

Other than the beating of his own heart, he heard nothing.

There was a purpose for the angles in the tunnels. They prevented the American soldiers from firing in a straight line, or throwing grenades.

*Is Charlie waiting around the corner?*

Billy wondered for a moment why he had volunteered. Forcing himself to control his bladder, he hugged the ground low and peered around quickly.

Nothing.

He breathed a sigh of relief and crawled forward.

It was after another hundred yards of crawling in fear that he came across his first booby-trap.

A three-step snake, so called because you took only three steps after being bitten.

The snake, a bamboo viper, was tied to a pole that was wedged into the floor. It was easy to miss, and if Billy hadn't been on hyperalert, he would have tripped it, and the reptile would have bitten him.

He shot it through the head and then held his breath as the sound rolled through the tunnel.

He hugged the ground, making himself as small as possible, expecting AK-47 fire from the VC.

None came.

Billy pushed on ahead, through more twists and turns, and suddenly the tunnel opened up into a room.

He got to standing height and moved to a corner, his handgun sweeping the open space.

Something flashed in his memory, something one of the Rats had said, and he jumped back just in time as punji sticks reared out of the wall.

He watched them, horrified, as they pierced the air and came to a stop, quivering.

*They would have ripped through my back.*

He retched and moved away from the corner, remembering what the other soldiers had told him.

*Stay away from corners. That's where they set their traps.*

He wiped his mouth with shaking fingers, planted more explosives, and crawled back into the tunnel.

He cleared out three more traps before turning back, his nerves deserting him.

The return was a blur. All he could remember was his fingers scraping at the hard clay, his breathing loud and harsh, as he slithered towards his exit.

Back at the hole, he struggled into the harness, praying that no VC appeared at this last moment.

And then his friends were hauling him up, and he was breathing fresh air, and it had never smelled so sweet.

Billy Patten had survived his first outing underground.

# Chapter 20

*Present Day*

Two days after the confrontation with Ken Farrell and Cole, Beth and Meghan Petersen were in Vietnam.

After the last of the US troops had pulled out in 1973, North Vietnamese troops had conquered South Vietnam, and Saigon had been renamed Ho Chi Minh City after the communist leader.

HCMC, as it was often called, was in the southeastern part of the country and was the largest city in the country, with a population of eight million.

Earlier in the day, they had been in Hanoi, the capital city, with Colonel General Cam Van Lanh of the Ministry of Public Security.

The senior officer was a deputy minister, and the second-highest executive in the department that oversaw the police forces in Vietnam.

In his late forties, Lanh was short in stature, with an unlined face and black eyes that never seemed to blink.

That bland expression had given way to warmth when the

twins had entered his office.

Zeb and the minister had history, a good one. Zeb had helped Lanh capture several drug runners on a previous mission.

Those big wins had nailed the colonel's career to the fast track, and he had been promoted to his current rank.

Lanh served them tea and listened patiently to their story. One eyebrow rose, and that was his only display of astonishment.

'You realize,' he said as he bowed and handed the cups to the sisters, 'that all this happened a long while ago. More than forty years! Finding someone who saw or remembers the tunnel accident will be hard.' He frowned, looking into space. 'I don't even know if there were witnesses. As to this person, Dang, that is a very common name in Vietnam. There will be millions in the country with that name.'

'Yes, sir,' Beth acknowledged. 'We were thinking of inquiring in Ho Chi Minh City. About witnesses, as well as Dang. Finding him might be easier, if such a person exists. He could have been a South Vietnamese soldier. Someone who was in contact with US forces. We know that Billy Patten's base was in Cu Chi.'

Lanh looked away and then picked up his phone. He spoke rapidly, then hung up and made another call. He was smiling when he finished.

'Kien Huy Thuc. He will help you.'

'He is—'

'Ho Chi Minh City's police chief. My friend.'

*I bet all police officers will claim to be his friend*, Meghan thought, suppressing a smile.

A two-hour flight brought them to HCMC, and forty minutes later, they were in the city's police headquarters on Tran Hung Dao Street.

Thuc looked similar to Lanh, except for a neatly trimmed mustache and greying hair.

He greeted them effusively, bowing a lot, and gave them a tour of the office. Anyone who had been sent by the minister had to be given the royal treatment.

Afterwards, he led them to a room that held a few chairs, a desk, and a computer. It had its own uniformed attendant, who sprang to attention and gave a salute when they entered.

'All records of South Vietnamese soldiers, there.' He waved expansively. 'Names. Addresses. Everything. An Khoi,' he said, nodding at the officer, 'will help you if you need anything.'

'All the records?' Beth asked dubiously.

'All that we have.' Thuc's smile faltered.

*Better than nothing*, Meghan told herself and silently indicated at her sister to accept Thuc's offer.

'What about witnesses?' Beth asked.

'Difficult. An Khoi will do his best, but very difficult.'

Three hours later, they yawned and stretched while An Khoi rushed over and poured more tea for them.

'Private school, ma'am.' The officer smiled when they complimented him on his English.

He had conjured up a list of people who knew about the tunnel accident. Officials, ambulance drivers, policemen and women.

Quite a few of those on the list had died. Many had moved away and lived in distant parts of the country.

An Khoi had made calls and had spoken to all those who were contactable.

A few of them remembered the accident, and they recollected one twin dying. However, not one of them could say which son was the survivor.

The Vietnamese police officer had then produced records of all South Vietnamese soldiers who had served with the Americans in Cu Chi.

The dossiers were extensive and were in Vietnamese, as well as in English. They had names, photographs, and occupations of those soldiers who had survived.

There were also over a hundred Dangs.

'Meghan and I will help out with the phone calls. Let's split the names up.' Beth divided the list and turned to An Khoi. 'We'll need some interpreters.'

Khoi returned with two female officers, who smiled and bowed too.

They bobbed their heads when Beth explained what was required, and while Khoi arranged for more phone lines and headsets, they studied the lists.

It was close to six pm when Beth called for a break.

They had whittled the Dangs down to five.

Each one of those Dangs had served closely with the Fifth Infantry Division, Billy Patten's unit.

None of the men were at home when the officers had called.

'We'll pay them a visit tomorrow,' Beth told An Khoi, who pointed an imperious finger at one of the officers.

'Hy Phuong will come with you. She will help. Those men will cooperate.'

*I bet they will. This is a communist country. Citizens will do what the state tells them.*

Meghan shook hands with Phuong and thanked An Khoi, while her sister made arrangements for the next day's visits.

The first two Dangs turned out to the wrong ones. Both of them were in their sixties, and one of them ran a chain of takeout restaurants, while another worked as an insurance salesman.

They remembered the war. Who didn't? They remembered the American base in Cu Chi, and each one of them brought out several photographs and talked about their memories at length.

However, neither of them knew Billy Patten.

The third Dang started off more promisingly.

'Yes,' he said, 'I knew Billy Patten. He and I went after VC. We killed many Charlie.

'He was big, and I felt like a dwarf next to him,' he laughed, revealing bad teeth.

Meghan sighed inwardly. *Billy Patten wasn't big.*

The fourth Dang wanted a reward for revealing any information he might have.

Hy Phuong rattled off a volley at him in Vietnamese, but Dang stood his ground. No reward, no talking.

She called An Khoi, who threatened Dang and promised all kinds of dire outcomes.

The Vietnamese cracked and said he didn't know Billy Patten.

The last Dang, Nang Quy Dang, lived in a white villa in District Two in HCMC.

It had a gated entrance and a security guard.

'Master is not here.' The guard stood implacably when Phuong displayed her credentials.

'I made an appointment with his secretary,' she insisted.

'Master is not here. Come again.' The guard wasn't yielding.

He didn't budge even when An Khoi came on the line and verbally tore a strip off him.

His master wasn't at home. There was no way he was going to open the gate.

'We will come back. You had better start looking for a job,' Phuong threatened in defeat.

'His secretary made an appointment. I don't know what happened,' she apologized as their driver took them back to their hotel.

Nang Quy Dang was an exporter of Vietnamese art. He had started off after the war by selling leftover American weapons and equipment.

There were several buyers who wanted artifacts of war, and Dang did very well.

As memories of the war faded, Dang graduated to selling art. He traveled to North Vietnam, procured handcrafted pottery from villages and sold it in South Vietnam. He sold South Vietnamese bric-a-brac in North Vietnam.

His reputation grew. He started importing silk from China and then hit the big time when he cultivated Vietnamese artists and exported their work.

The police had a file on him, as they did on every wealthy individual in the city. It was a communist country, after all.

Dang had fought alongside US soldiers. He had gone out on seek-and-destroy missions with the Fifth Infantry Division.

The Petersens had called other survivors of the unit, and many of them had identified Dang. It was quite possible that Nang Quy Dang was the Dang Billy Patten had scribbled about.

However, they had to speak to him to confirm that.

They left voicemail messages for him and waited.

Dang didn't return their call.

They set out to the Cu Chi tunnels, at the Ben Duoc site, the next day, with Hy Phuong accompanying them. An Khoi stayed back to make progress on the hunt for the tunnel accident's witnesses.

The Cu Chi underground network, northwest of the main city, was comprised of one hundred and twenty kilometers of underground passages.

The complex of tunnels had another tourist entrance, at Ben Dinh, where the passages had been enlarged and reconstructed.

The entire region was now a visitor attraction, and the tunnels themselves had been turned into a war museum. It had shooting ranges and displays of war weapons, and memorabilia that could be purchased.

An Khoi met them after they finished their visit.

'This isn't where it happened.'

# Chapter 21

'This wasn't where the accident happened? Where they died?' Beth repeated, dumbfounded.

'No, ma'am. Some tunnels collapsed here, but no one died. Your client's father didn't die here.'

Beth stared at Meghan, who shrugged. Ken Farrell had given them explicit details about where the accident had happened.

Tunnel Ten, in the Cu Chi complex. He had been clear about its location, and its entrance. The tunnel had been part of the tourist attraction but was now closed.

An Khoi looked embarrassed and cast a glance around him to confirm that they were alone.

'That is what we told everyone, that the accident had happened in Tunnel Ten. The newspapers, even Mr. Patten's family, and his lawyers, they got the same story. I spoke to Colonel General Lanh. He agreed that we should tell you the real location. It is further away.'

'Why the secrecy?' Beth was intrigued. 'These tunnels are old. It's not as if accidents wouldn't happen.'

'It was not my decision, ma'am. I wasn't even born then.

The colonel general told me it was because we didn't want the accident site to become another tourist attraction. And also, we were ashamed. We didn't want a bad image.'

Meghan considered it for a few moments. *Plausible. A communist country likes to present its best face to the world. We'll dig into it, however.*

An Khoi drove them in his police vehicle after dismissing Hy Phuong.

'No luck with witnesses,' he told them. 'I don't think we will find any. The records of that accident are sketchy. It doesn't look like there was anyone else in the tunnel other than Billy Patten and his two sons,' he explained as he led them away from Ben Douc, heading east.

Meghan pictured the region in her mind. Ben Dinh was to the southeast of Ben Duoc and was very close to Saigon River, whereas the site they had been to was further away from the main city.

An Khoi didn't head to Ben Dinh. He continued going towards the river, and when they were a few miles from it, he went off-road, taking a dirt track that had a No Entry sign on it, in Vietnamese and in English.

Beth, who was sitting in the front with him, flicked a glance at her sister, towards Meghan's jacket.

Meghan nodded imperceptibly. She was armed. Her Glock was in her shoulder holster, spare mags in her pockets.

They trusted An Khoi, but they didn't know where he was taking them.

Their questions were answered when the officer braked to a halt after another half an hour of driving.

They were in a clearing, surrounded by dense bamboo

trees. A hut that was blown away by the wind. The ever-present plastic bags and empty water bottles littered the ground.

'That way.' An Khoi pointed and took them down a barely-there track in the forest.

A fifteen-minute trek brought them to another clearing.

'There was a village there, once.' He pointed in the direction of the river. 'A mile away. No longer exists. It was bombed by the Americans.'

A shocked expression appeared on his face. 'I didn't mean—'

'That's alright. The war was a long time ago,' Beth told him kindly.

'The forest was regrown in this area. No traces of the village remain.'

'What's here?' Meghan placed her hands on her hips and looked around.

An Khoi's eyes twinkled. 'This, ma'am, is still part of the tunnels. There's an entrance here. Can you see it?'

The sisters narrowed their eyes and sectioned each part of the clearing, the way Zeb had taught them.

A termite mound. Another track leading into the jungle. Plastic trash. A faint depression, like old vehicle tracks. But nothing like a trapdoor, a hole in the ground, or anything remotely looking like a tunnel.

An Khoi laughed at their expressions. 'That is why the Viet Cong were so successful. They were masters at deception.'

He strode to the termite mound and knocked the mud away with a fist.

He scraped the loose soil away with his shoes and pointed to a wooden door set in the soil.

It was padlocked and had another No Entry sign.

'Down there. That is where Billy Patten and his son died. His surviving son was found outside the hole, dazed, with no recollection of how he had escaped or what had happened.'

Beth crouched down and fingered the door. it was flush with the ground, the same color as the surrounding surface.

Cakes of mud stuck to it in places, and a few shoots of grass thrust out.

'It is larger than the original doors,' the police officer continued. 'I read some of the files back in the office. We think it was widened, and even the tunnels below it were made bigger.'

'Why?'

'We don't know. We interviewed several people. carried out a thorough investigation. But no one knows.'

'Maybe they didn't tell you?' Meghan offered.

'That's highly unlikely.' An Khoi went to his vehicle and removed a black plastic sack. He collected and bagged the trash around the site and tossed the sack in the rear of the SUV. 'Very few people lie to us. If they are found out, it won't be pleasant for them.'

Meghan didn't reply, knowing what he said was true. *In such a country, only the rich or those with lawyers can afford to lie. The police wouldn't have questioned such people. They would have asked the tunnel diggers, the peasants, the surviving VC soldiers.*

Beth wandered off into the jungle to explore the area. After rustling around, she returned.

'There must be more holes. All these tunnels had more than one exit.'

'You are correct, ma'am. But all have been sealed by us.'

They followed him to the river, down the trail they had seen earlier. He left the track and pushed through dense undergrowth, and near another clearing, he scraped through dirt and pointed to another door.

It too was sealed.

'You don't need directions?' Beth squinted at him, not hiding the suspicious note in her voice.

An Khoi held up his wrist in answer and turned it over to face them.

He was wearing a smartwatch on which was a map. 'I don't need them, ma'am. Technology,' he deadpanned.

They went to three more holes in a two-mile radius, both of them sealed, and then returned to the vehicle.

'Why did Billy Patten come here?' Beth wondered aloud and got a shrug from An Khoi.

'I don't think we will ever find an answer to that, ma'am. It's possible he went underground in this particular network and wanted to show it to his sons.'

'The story that Cole Patten and his lawyer told us—that he was found outside Tunnel Ten, with quite a few witnesses, and someone took him to hospital. That was deliberate misinformation, too?

'Yes. Taking him to hospital was correct. But there were no witnesses. A farmer found him, called the police and an ambulance. We have already spoken to the surviving police officials and the ambulance and hospital staff. They don't remember anything. The farmer is dead.' An Khoi had the grace to look embarrassed.

The Petersens were silent on the way back, knowing they didn't have many more leads to pursue.

Meghan's cell rang as they were entering the hotel after An Khoi had dropped them off.

She glanced at the number and lifted a finger to silence her sister, who was ready to fire a question.

She put the phone on speaker, and a familiar voice came on. Debbie, the receptionist at the nursing home in Fredericksburg.

'I asked Leroy about Dang, just as you requested,' she said without preamble. They could hear voices in the background, and the faint sounds of an ambulance. 'He went into the past and started talking about Brenda. I tried again, and this time he started talking about Josh Patten. How nice a boy he was. The only visitor he had. On the third attempt, he started talking about Pete Garrett.'

'Can you try again?' Meghan asked hesitantly. She wasn't surprised when a firm *no* came back.

'You have to understand,' Debbie said, softening, 'Leroy's well-being is more important to me than your hunt.'

'We do, Debbie.' Meghan thanked her and dialed another number.

'Who are you calling?'

'Pete Garrett. We should have tried him in the first place.'

Before her call connected, a short, bald, bespectacled man approached them.

He was well-dressed in a suit, his black shoes gleaming. Lean physique, only the wrinkles on his face indicating he was in his sixties. Behind him was another Vietnamese, carrying a briefcase.

'Beth Petersen? Meghan Petersen?' he asked in accented English.

'I'm Meghan.' She canceled the outgoing call.

'I am Nang Quy Dang.'

# Chapter 22

Meghan checked out the lobby instinctively, feeling Beth move away from behind her.

It was an upmarket hotel with its own security system. It catered to a Western clientele. Men in suits were normal, as were formally attired couples.

No sign of any gun-toting thugs. No outline of a weapon on the suit behind Dang.

'I heard you have been looking for me.'

'You missed our appointment, Mr. Dang.'

'I am here now.' He made no apology for his absence and pointed to an alcove that was empty. 'Shall we?'

'What was your relationship with Billy Patten, Mr. Dang?' she asked once they were seated.

'I don't know any Billy Patten.'

She stared at him. 'Mr. Dang, you were in the Vietnam War—'

'We call it the American War, in this country,' he interrupted, his tone factual. He wasn't rude. His eyes met hers squarely. 'I got the voicemail someone from the HCMC police left for me. I was traveling. My EA,' he said, jerking his head in the suit's direction, 'accepted the appointment by mistake.'

'We're searching for someone who knew Billy Patten. He was with the Fifth Infantry. On the Cu Chi American base. You went on missions with them,' she stated.

*Ball's in your court, buddy. You'll either deny or confirm.*

Dang went for the first option.

'I didn't come across Billy Patten. There were many American soldiers, many battalions. It was many years ago.'

'Who do you remember?'

'Why do you need to know? Who is this Billy Patten?'

*How much do we tell him?*

He seemed to read her thoughts. 'Ms. Petersen, I am a businessman. The fact that you got the police to set up an appointment tells me two things. One is that you are well connected. Secondly, if the police could have helped you, they would have. So, this isn't a criminal matter, or a war crimes matter. A civil matter, probably? In your country?'

Meghan was impressed but didn't show it.

*Smart. He's very smart. That reference to our connections...he knows if he doesn't cooperate, the police can make life hard for him.*

'Billy Patten was a Tunnel Rat. You're right. There's a development back home concerning him. We've been hired by his family to talk to those who knew him here.'

'He's no more?'

'No, sir. He died. In this country, in a tunnel accident.'

She outlined the incident quickly, watching his face for any giveaways. There were none. No flashing of eyes. No tics. No looking away.

'I am a good poker player, Ms. Petersen,' he said blandly.

'You are.'

'I don't remember that accident either, but that month, I was in China. I wasn't paying much attention to what went on back home.'

'Mr. Dang.' Beth pinned him down with her eyes, her voice cool. 'Why should we believe you didn't know Patten?'

'I was in Saigon those days, but nowhere near Cu Chi. My commander is still alive. You can ask him. You can ask the other soldiers in my unit. I have nothing to hide.'

He rattled off a series of names and waited for them to take notes.

'You have a good memory?' he asked when neither sister made a move towards pen or paper.

'No need, Mr. Dang.' Meghan smiled wolfishly and held her cell up. 'You're being recorded.'

The Vietnamese left shortly with no further insight.

'What do you think?' Meghan asked as she headed to the elevator and pressed the button to their floor.

'He's not our Dang.'

'Why do you say so?'

'Those names. He gave them out readily. He might be in a position of wealth, but you can bet not many of his fellow soldiers are. It'd be far too easy for the cops to lean on him and get the truth.'

'My smarts are rubbing off on you.'

The sisters were in their late twenties. However, that didn't stop Beth from sticking her tongue out at her twin.

Meghan stopped abruptly in the hallway leading to their rooms.

'Garrett,' she explained and dug out her phone.

They got Pete Garrett on the second ring, and after he had listened to them, he sighed.

'Nope, I don't know any Dang either. However, maybe, just maybe, I might know someone who does.'

'Who, sir?' Meghan aimed dagger eyes at her sister, who was fist-pumping silently.

'Luc Cham. He was in the SVA, the South Vietnamese Army. I remembered him after our last call. He was in their Seventh Infantry and came out with us on sweeps. He, a few others, and us. We got close. Shared cigarettes, chocolates. That kind of stuff. If we had a Vietnamese friend, it was Cham.'

'Would he be alive, sir?'

'Yeah. Got a card from him just a few months back. Hold on. I'll search for it.'

'Got a pen?'

'Yes, sir.'

*He doesn't need to know we're recording this.*

'He owns fields, just outside Sa Dec. That's about three hours from HCMC. You want me to tell him you'll be visiting?'

'Yes, sir. And if you can share his number…'

'Sure.'

They went for a run the next day, just as the sun rose and turned Ho Chi Minh City to gold.

Past tree-lined avenues, down sidewalks, as motorcycles whizzed past on the street. They passed high-rises and rows of stores. Flower vendors on the street, hawkers who sold cheap trinkets to tourists.

The Western world's influence could be seen in Vietnam, but surrounded and modified by local culture and by history. Young men turned to look at them, two American women in their youth, their brown hair bouncing on their backs, headbands on their foreheads, shades on their faces, jackets concealing the ever-present Glocks.

They returned to the hotel an hour later to shower, and when they went down to the lobby, An Khoi was waiting for them.

He was in his uniform, drawing curious looks from guests and deferential reverence from the hotel staff.

'My staff will be working one more day on witnesses. If we don't make any progress today, I will have to reassign them,' he told them awkwardly as he shook their hands.

*Can't blame him*, Meghan thought. 'We understand, An Khoi. Maybe our luck will change at Sa Dec.'

He snapped a salute, bowed grandly, and held the door open for them.

They had called him after finishing with Pete Garrett the previous evening, and the officer had volunteered to drive them.

The sisters had accepted his offer. They needed someone who spoke the language, and his presence would help break down any resistance.

The officer kept a commentary going as he drove out of the city, all traffic falling away from his police vehicle.

Sa Dec was almost at the center of the Mekong Delta, a region of fifteen thousand square miles, where the Mekong River emptied in the sea.

It was the rice bowl of the country and had urban developments coexisting with sleepy villages that time had forgotten.

Buffalo slumbered in paddy fields, rice and fruit-filled boats plied the many tributaries in the region.

They stopped once to refresh themselves and were immediately surrounded by coconut vendors.

Meghan brushed perspiration away from her forehead as she sipped from a freshly opened coconut.

'You think he'll cooperate?' she asked their guide.

An Khoi looked down at his uniform. 'I would say so, ma'am.'

They reached Luc Cham's home at lunchtime, a three-story house painted yellow on the outside, a sloping tile roof on top, and a strip of pavement that ran to the street.

A gap-toothed man in a loose shirt and trousers greeted them when they alighted.

'Luc Cham,' An Khoi introduced him.

Cham folded his hands in greeting and gestured towards the house.

The inside of the house had a high ceiling, a fan turning lazily to create a breeze.

Cham went into the depths of the house and returned with glasses of coconut water on a tray. An elderly woman followed him, bearing plates of rice and fish.

'Eat. Eat.' Cham made a motion with his fingers, grinning widely.

'It would be disrespectful—'

'I get it, An Khoi,' Meghan told him and tucked into her food.

An hour later, Cham began to speak. He fingered the photographs on Meghan's phone, his face ruminative, his eyes seeing into a past only he had experienced.

Yes, he knew Billy Patten. He called out to his wife, and she returned with a metal box.

He opened it to show empty packs of cigarettes. Lucky Strikes, Camels, a pack of C-rations, a lighter.

Cham fingered them lovingly, his eyes moist, his voice breaking.

'We lost many people. All sides,' An Khoi translated quietly, hearing the war come alive in the old man's voice. 'Even Americans. They sent me to reeducation camp. My wife was alone. Pregnant. Our son died during childbirth. No one came to help her. I came back. I had these fields from my father. I live quietly now.'

'Pete.' His face lightened. 'Good friend. Very good friend.'

He yelled out again, and his wife returned with a bundle of letters and cards.

'Pete,' he announced proudly, pointing with a wrinkled finger. 'A friend translates his letters for me.

'Billy, brave. Went in tunnels. Killed many VC. But different.' He shook his head.

'How was he different?' Beth asked.

'Different,' Cham said insistently. 'Not like other soldiers. I was not very close to him. Pete and Leroy. Good friends. Not like Billy.'

Beth made to press him, but Meghan stopped her. *Let's find out about why we're here*.

'Did you know one Dang, sir?'

'Dang?'

'Yes, sir. Dang. I think he knew Billy. Maybe you knew him too.'

'Dang…' Cham trailed off. His face darkened and his fingers shook.

He stuffed the cigarette packs back into the box. Retied the string around the letters.

'Dang. No. Don't know him.'

And with that, he strode off to an inner room and didn't emerge.

# Chapter 23

*Vietnam, 1967*

The second time Billy went into a hole, he knew he had changed.

He didn't know how, exactly. He still felt fear. His belly still clenched when he climbed down, not knowing if Charlie was waiting.

It was when he was prone, crawling slowly, that it came to him.

He viewed his friends, especially Leroy and Pete, differently. He had been deep below the ground. They hadn't. Billy thought that experience marked him. He wasn't like them.

*Focus*, he told himself. *Charlie will like nothing better than for you to be distracted.*

After his first *ride*—that was what he called it to himself—he had met the other Rats on the base. There weren't many of them. Five. There had been six, but VC had gotten to one of them.

He found a closer camaraderie existed among the Rats than the other soldiers.

*I'm one of them now.*

He inched forward, smelling the stale air, his eyes searching the hard floor, the walls, and straight ahead.

His flashlight illuminated just a few feet ahead of him. He had to rely on his other senses to detect the presence of Charlie.

Some of the Rats wore gas masks because trapped fumes inside the passages could be deadly. However, Billy chose to take his chances without one.

He also preferred to go down alone, in contrast to some other Rats who worked in pairs.

*Not that there are any more volunteers in my unit.*

His smile faded when he thought he heard a noise.

He stopped, adrenaline surging inside him, his heart thumping so loud that he thought it could be heard by the VC.

He heard it again. A slight noise, like the brush of cloth on wall.

Ahead of him, just past the bend in the tunnel.

His flashlight didn't cast its light that far. The curve was still in the dark from his side.

He carefully flicked off the light and clenched it between his teeth.

Raised his handgun, steeled himself, and leaped forward.

*One VC. No, two!* Crawling right at him. Their eyes widening.

Billy didn't think. Didn't call out.

He triggered as rapidly as he could. Once, twice, three times, and then he retreated past the bend and tossed a grenade.

He reloaded quickly under the cover of the blast and moved further back.

There could be Charlie on the other side of the wall. They could pierce him.

He lay still, sweating, his leg twitching involuntarily, his gun ready, his eyes as wide open as he could make them.

No VC appeared. No spear went through his flesh.

He wiped his forehead on his sleeve and resumed his crawl.

Didn't look at the bodies. Climbed over them and trailed where the VC had come from.

It was a room. Wide and tall enough for him to stand hunched.

It seemed to be a planning room of some kind.

There was a rough wooden table. A hand-drawn map.

Billy grabbed it. Searched the room carefully, staying away from corners.

There were some pots and pans. Bricks, firewood and matchsticks.

He placed detonators and went back to the passage.

He spent another hour in the tunnel, encountering no other VC.

He then went back to his hole, donned the harness, and climbed back up before setting off the detonators.

'Any trouble?' Leroy asked him, a concerned look on his face.

'Nah,' Billy replied. He was a Rat. Rats ate trouble for breakfast and didn't even burp.

Templeman took the map from him, studied it for a moment and patted him on his back.

Billy swelled with pride. That gesture meant more than a medal.

In the evening, as his friends gathered around a hut and shared smokes and stories, Billy stood to the side. He didn't speak much, laughed when the others laughed. One of the men made a joke about Charlie. Billy didn't join in. He thought he should feel anger at the VC, but he didn't.

He stopped thinking, allowed himself to relax and guffawed genuinely when Leroy told a good one.

Billy went on more rides. He was getting better at detecting traps and VC.

That didn't mean he didn't have scares.

A spear scraped along his back one time. Another inch or two and it would have run through him.

He had fired rapidly at the clay wall and crawled ahead as quickly as he could, and when he was safely around a bend, he'd tossed two grenades.

He never saw those attackers.

He saw other VC, however.

Another time, two of them came rushing at him as he was exploring another room.

It was the slap of feet on the floor that alerted him.

He sprang away, his gun swinging up, firing from the hip.

He crashed against the wall, fell to the floor, and rolled desperately, evading the pungi stakes that sprang from the floor.

He managed to get out of that tunnel with just scrapes and nicks, and for the first time, he felt satisfaction in demolishing it, and the VC in it.

It was three months later that his life changed again.

They were searching a village near the Saigon River, several klicks south of Ben Dinh, five miles from their base.

They had found VC and had finished them. As they were

leaving, more Charlie had emerged from the jungle and fired on them.

'Fall back,' Templeman roared.

They obeyed him, fleeing, returning fire as quickly as they could. Leroy called for air support on his radio, and just as they reached the tree line, away from their attackers, the first gunship arrived.

Billy paused for a few moments to watch the destruction.

Rockets blazed from the choppers and tore at the forest. He could see explosions and hear human cries. He saw bodies tossed up, and then Leroy yelled at him to get his ass back.

Billy stumbled away, following, his eyes ahead of him.

He fell. Thought VC had gotten to him, but when he looked back, there were no Charlie.

Only the jungle, and the sounds of the gunships.

He searched the ground, seeking what had tripped him.

No branches. No roots.

He was in a clearing, and as he bent closer, he saw it.

A trapdoor.

Billy frowned.

The holes were usually close to villages. He knew this was a new hole.

He hurriedly marked the spot and joined his friends, and they fled back to safety.

He didn't mention the entrance to anyone. He didn't know why and didn't bother to analyze himself.

He made a flimsy excuse to Templeman the next day, that he and the other Rats were checking out tunnels near that village, and went back to the area.

He knew his sarge didn't buy his explanation, but Billy had

more than enough in the goodwill bank. Templeman didn't question him in any detail, and it helped that the sergeant was distracted.

Billy didn't tell Leroy or Pete where he was going.

He ran at a fast pace, keeping an eye out for VC. It wouldn't do if he got himself killed when he was on alone time.

He reached the trapdoor and stopped for a few moments, breathing heavily.

He surveyed the area. No sign of Charlie.

He went forward and opened the door.

It swung back easily.

He tied a rope to a nearby tree and lowered himself, his heart in his mouth.

The tunnel was no different from others he had seen, but there seemed to be a peculiar smell that he hadn't encountered before.

He tried to place it, but he couldn't.

He filed it away in his mind and crawled forward.

Checked out several twists and turns and went through many branches. He drew small marks on the walls to guide him on his return trip.

He reached a larger room and stood for a while, observing it.

It was empty. No table. No sign of cooking. It seemed to be a gathering place for no specific purpose.

The walls seemed to be of a different mud, but in the dimness, he couldn't make much out.

Billy checked out traps, and when he was turning back, his jacket swiped the wall.

Something clicked.

He dove away, suspecting a pungi trap.

There wasn't one. There was nothing.

*What clicked?*

He looked even more carefully. No vipers. No bamboo sticks. He tapped the wall lightly. It sounded like any other.

He pushed and pressed the area where the click had come from, and suddenly, a trapdoor opened.

It was shoulder-height, and beyond it was darkness.

He turned on his flashlight and gaped.

Rows of sacks, neatly mounted on top of one another. The trapdoor hid a storage area of some kind. Not a room, more of a locker.

There was no way to enter it. One had to reach out and withdraw the sacks, one by one.

Billy pulled out one sack. It was two feet in length, one foot wide, several pounds in weight.

He ripped one open and gawked for the second time.

Powder. Creamy in color. Crystalline in feel.

# Chapter 24

*Raw heroin, H.* It came to him suddenly. The Golden Triangle, a region that included northern Thailand, Laos, and Burma, was one of the biggest producers of opium.

There were always rumors that the VC traded in illegal drugs to fund their war.

Billy didn't believe in those whispers. All the VC they had captured and interrogated, junior as well as senior officers, had vehemently denied such allegations.

*It wouldn't benefit them. Their own soldiers could get hooked.*

*Nope, this has to be some rogue operator who's using the tunnel for storage.*

He flashed back to the passages, rooms, and levels he had checked out.

No, there wasn't a factory in the tunnel. Not that he had seen.

*Maybe just a store? A factory would require people. They would be noticed by other VC.*

Billy leaned inside the opening and drew out more sacks and discovered more powder.

There was a second layer of sacks behind the first. He reached and brought out the uppermost one.

It felt different. Not hard, like the ones containing H.

He ripped one open and sagged on his heels. He felt faint, his breathing stuttered.

The sack was stuffed with US currency, all of them Benjamins, hundred-dollar bills.

Billy dipped his hand inside and drew them out, letting them flutter to the floor in disbelief.

They were real. Genuine. He drew out his wallet and compared bills.

Yeah. He was no expert, but these were the real deal.

Awareness returned to him.

He was in a VC tunnel. Charlie could appear anytime. The rogue operator whose stash this was could come.

Billy swiftly checked out more sacks and found three more packed with currency.

He hauled the four Benjamin-laden bags to the bottom of the hole.

It took time, and he was a nervous wreck by the time he had finished.

He went back to the trapdoor, placed the H-sacks back inside, closed it, wiped his traces away as well as he could, and went back to the entrance.

He had to make three trips to carry the sacks out.

He took cover in the jungle and waited for his pulse to slow down, his harsh breathing to even out, his sweat to dry.

He started thinking clearly.

He didn't know how much money there was in the sacks.

Tens of thousands for sure. Whoever it belonged to would be one angry VC.

*You can come after me, Charlie. This is a game I can play.*

Billy hauled the sacks close to his camp. It took two trips, but he wasn't complaining. Not with the contents of those bags.

He crawled towards the outhouses near his camp, held his breath at the stench, and dug into the soil rapidly.

He buried the sacks deep inside before covering it, noting its location until it was burned in his mind, and then went back into the jungle.

He went down another hole, all by himself, swept it, and demolished it.

He returned to his camp in the evening, trying to keep a straight face, and joined his friends.

Leroy looked at him questioningly.

'Just some Rats work. A few tunnels,' he answered, taking the mug of coffee his friend offered.

Billy had crossed a line.

He knew it. He didn't care.

Billy got lucky the next day. Their unit continued their search-and-destroy missions along the river, clearing villages, going into the jungle after Charlie.

He got one glimpse of the tunnel's door, and from an almost invisible mark he had made, he knew no one else had entered it.

He went to the hole in the night.

No Rat had ever attempted a night excursion. Billy knew he would be the first. However, this time, he wasn't hunting VC.

The jungle was dark when he reached the hole and waited for several moments to check the scene out.

No disturbance.

In the distance, he heard the sounds of the river and could smell the burning village they had bombed in the day. A light breeze carried the stench of rotting flesh.

Billy had gotten used to the smells and sounds in 'Nam. They no longer bothered him.

He opened the trapdoor and rappelled down the rope.

His gun was in his hand, his flashlight between his teeth.

On the tunnel's floor, he lay down and began the slow crawl. He was alert, watchful. Just because the NVA had shown no signs of their presence didn't mean VC weren't in the tunnel.

There were no enemy soldiers, however.

He went to the hidden door, removed it, and pulled out more sacks. He wasn't interested in the drugs. He was after Benjamins.

He got four sacks that night, and when he emerged in the forest, only two bags of currency were left in the tunnel.

He buried the four new sacks near the outhouse, made a show of circling their camp, in case anyone was watching, and headed back to his quarters.

He was lying down on his bed when a voice spoke.

Leroy's.

He froze.

'Billy, whatever you're doing, it doesn't feel right.'

Billy didn't answer his friend, and Leroy didn't pursue the matter. However, Billy sensed a coolness in his friend from that night onwards. Not just in him, but in Pete too.

It surprised him that the separation didn't bother him.

It was on his third sortie into the tunnel that Billy's life pivoted further.

He was crawling towards the room when he heard a noise.

He stopped, raised his handgun, and turned off his flashlight.

He widened his eyes, peering through the gloom.

*VC. At least one of them*, he made out from the sounds.

He wiped sweat off his palms, careful not to make any noise, and resumed.

He could take cover just before the bend and pour lead into the room.

If there were several VC, he would chuck grenades.

His six was clear, so he could escape if he was attacked from the front.

Decision made, he moved faster.

The sounds were clearer now. One voice, growling.

Billy knew only a few Vietnamese words, most of which were curses.

The VC was swearing.

He risked a peek around the bend.

One soldier, in VC uniform. Hands on hips, staring at the hole in the wall. Two flashlights on the floor, illuminating the room.

Sacks on the floor.

The soldier smacked a hand on his thigh and poked his head through the trapdoor. Removed it after a while and commenced shouting.

*He's alone. That's why he's loud.*

Billy watched for a while as the VC ripped several racks, spraying H on the floor carelessly.

He raised his head to swear in anger when Billy got to his

feet and entered the room.

The VC watched in disbelief for a moment and then dove at his AK-47, which was on the floor.

Billy shot him in the left thigh and kicked the rifle away.

He leaned down, punched him in the face, almost knocking him out, and searched the VC quickly. He found a knife, a few loose bills, nothing else.

The VC lay moaning on the floor, clutching his leg. Billy knew it wasn't a fatal wound. He knew where his round had entered.

The soldier was bald and small in stature, shorter than Billy by a couple of inches. He was clean-shaven, wore glasses, and had an ascetic look about him.

He seemed to be the same age as Billy.

'This is yours?' Billy asked him as the VC propped himself up and leaned against a wall, sweat pouring down his face.

The soldier didn't answer. He ripped a length of cloth off his shirt and made a rough tourniquet that he applied to his thigh.

'You.' Billy waited until the soldier had finished. 'This is your stash?'

The VC looked at him finally, meeting his eyes. There was a speculative look on his face.

There had to be a reason the American soldier hadn't killed him.

He introduced himself.

'I am Chieu Ton Dang.'

# Chapter 25

'You got my money,' Dang rasped, eyeing the AK-47 at Billy's feet.

'I got someone's money.' Billy grinned, confidence flooding him. He was a born salesman. He could sniff opportunity a mile away. There was a deal to be struck here.

'Mine,' Dang hissed and rolled towards him swiftly.

Billy backhanded him and the VC fell away, his mouth bleeding.

'Now it's mine. I can kill you and take everything. Leave your body here.'

He let the words sink in, saw the VC soldier translate them mentally, process them.

'I am still alive,' Dang responded after a while.

'You know why?'

Dang's eyes were dark, fathomless pools as he took in his American captor. A light burned in them when he connected the dots.

'You, greedy. Americans, greedy.'

The laugh burst from Billy, bringing tears to his eyes.

'You're right, buddy. I can kill you and take everything. I

can torture you and find out if there's more. However, the way I figure it, keeping you alive helps us both.'

Dang took a while to understand his words.

He shook his head. 'I find you. I kill you.'

'Your money will still be missing.'

'I find you. I torture you.'

'Not going to happen.'

'I tell other Charlie. We attack your camp.'

'That won't happen either. I can get our unit to attack you, raze your village.'

'What you offering?' Dang panted after exhausting all his options.

Billy tossed him his canteen, and after the VC had drunk his fill, he spoke.

'A partnership.'

Billy knew the risk he was taking. He didn't know Dang. The VC could kill him. He could bring more Charlie with him, hunt Billy and capture him.

*I could do the same to him too, however. I have the upper hand. Besides, I have most of his money.*

The Benjamins were Billy's aces.

As long as they were in his possession, he was confident Dang would listen to him.

However, he knew the VC would always be looking for a way to best him.

*That's not in his interest. Nor in mine.*

Billy saw it clearly in his mind.

If Dang could operate an illegal drug-running enterprise in the middle of the Vietnam War, under the noses of the Americans and his fellow VC, he had smarts.

Billy didn't lack in them either.

'Think big.' He crouched next to the VC, searching for simple English words that Dang would understand.

'I kill you, I keep the money. You kill me, you may get your money back. But if we both work together, we can get more. So much more.'

Dang didn't speak. He moistened his lips and eased his thigh.

*Dude's got a round in his leg. It's got to be hurting like hell, but he's not crying. Got to hand it to him. He's got nerve.*

'You sell your H in villages, don't you? You supply VC soldiers, Americans, whoever needs it. You got a network, don't you?'

Dang's face remained blank.

Billy sighed. It would be a long night. He used smaller words, easier ones.

Dang hesitated, and then nodded fractionally.

'This is your only cache?'

Dang blinked.

'Your only store?'

Dang shook his head.

'I thought not. How many of the others have been destroyed? By our Hueys, or in our raids?'

Dang held up four fingers.

'I can help.'

Billy could warn Dang of upcoming bombing runs or search-and-destroy missions. That would give the Vietnamese time to move his H stashes.

Billy could also point out other American soldiers and units, those who used. Dang's network could reach out to them, push them the drugs.

'You and me, we can make this big. You've done well to build this operation and get it to this stage. You want to become a king?'

'You got to trust me for that,' Billy said softly.

'You got my money. You asking me to trust you?' Dang sneered.

'Yeah. Because you'll kill me once I give you the money.'

'Other VC will kill you anyway.'

'I'm a Tunnel Rat. I don't die easily.'

They traded words back and forth, but Billy knew Dang was thinking furiously.

*He doesn't have a choice. I haven't killed him; that's one sign that he can trust me.*

'Tomorrow, we bomb two villages,' Billy offered. He drew a map on the floor and marked the locations. 'You can see if I'm lying tomorrow.'

Dang compressed his lips, staring at the map, saying nothing.

'Tomorrow evening. Seven pm. We'll meet here. At the top. We can talk further.'

He took the AK-47 with him and got to his feet. He pointed it at the VC momentarily and chuckled at the fear that flashed across Dang's face.

'I told you, I won't kill you. You gotta believe me.'

He went out of the room, and when he was back in the tunnel, he tossed the rifle back.

'Tomorrow. Seven pm.' he repeated. 'And watch out for those villages.'

*Present Day*

'Who is Dang?' Gorbunov asked irritably.

He was in his New York apartment, watching Chisholm's stock chart.

He was buying carefully, stealthily, using several shell companies to execute his trades.

The market knew that he was circling the steel corporation and also knew he had a small position. If it knew just how he was buying, and how much, the share price would go up. That wasn't what he wanted.

'I am finding out,' Kirilov answered.

His killer had followed the sisters to Vietnam, getting close enough to them at some hotel to overhear snatches of their conversation.

'Find out fast. We need to know what they are up to.'

Kirilov hung up.

Gorbunov's killer sat in a restaurant, watching the hotel where the sisters were staying.

He had followed them to the Mekong Delta and had noted the house they had gone into.

He had made inquiries and found out they had met with Luc Cham, then made further inquiries and found out who Cham was.

That told him the twins were on Dang's trail. Kirilov ordered another cup of tea and drank the hot, sweet beverage slowly.

He would sit back and let the twins do the running around. Once they found who Dang was and located him, Kirilov would act.

His lizard-like eyes swept over the street outside.

He didn't see any sign of Carter or those two men, the black one and the blond one.

However, he knew the three men were in Vietnam.

He knew their kind. They would protect the women.

They weren't a threat as yet.

And even if they were, Kirilov could take them out.

'Where are you?'

'You gotta get your hearing checked, Zeb.' Bwana snorted in disgust. 'Or your memory. You're getting old. We told you. We're tailing Beth and Meg. They went to some village. We followed them. We're outside their hotel now.'

'They know you're there?'

'Nope. Give us some credit, for Chrissakes,' he protested in an aggrieved tone. 'Say,' he asked suspiciously, 'where are you?'

'New York. If you're with the twins, I'm not needed. You two can stop a nuclear war. Or start one.'

Zeb hung up and tossed his cell onto the seat next to him.

He wasn't in New York. He was in a white car, a taxi, that had the logo of a cab company. He wore a simple white shirt and khakis.

He was posing as a cab driver in Ho Chi Minh City.

He knew he would stand out as a Westerner, but he didn't intend to take any passengers.

He was five hundred yards away from Kirilov's café. He had his binos with him, and his Glock. His screen told him where the Petersens and Bwana and Roger were.

He had only one goal—to keep Kirilov in his sights.

He waited and watched. He was good at both. He was now finding that the Russian killer, too, was good at the two activities. As good as Zeb.

An Khoi picked up the sisters from their hotel and drove them to the police station.

He told them he had cajoled and threatened Luc Cham and had pleaded with his wife, but the Vietnamese farmer hadn't emerged from his room.

Neither had he responded to any more questions.

'He knows Dang.' An Khoi had thumped the wheel in frustration as he had driven back from Sa Dec.

'Yeah. We'll have to find some other way to find out who Dang is,' Beth had replied.

Werner hadn't come up with any answers. The supercomputer was still digging into the Patten family's lives, and that search wasn't turning productive either.

An Khoi didn't have any better news on the witness front either. He had suspended the search, and his team had gone back to their normal duties.

In the office that the Vietnamese police had assigned to them, Beth listlessly punched keys on the police computer, running random searches.

'You got any ideas?' she asked her sister.

Meghan didn't reply.

'I'm talking to you, not the wall.'

Still no response.

She swiveled her chair around to let fly a volley, and then bit it back.

Meghan had that expression, the one that said she was on to something.

'What?' She shook her twin's shoulder.

Meghan started. 'You remember what Duhan said?'

'He spoke a lot,' Beth replied impatiently. 'What are you referring to?'

'He said something about Billy. That he had spoken to Billy Patten after he had come back.'

'Yeah, what about it?'

'We assumed that meant he and Patten had spoken on their return from Vietnam.'

Beth saw where her sister was going.

'What if Patten visited this country on his own? After leaving the Army.'

# Chapter 26

Meghan waited till evening to make the call to Debbie.

'I can try,' the receptionist answered doubtfully. 'That's all you want to know? If Billy Patten had been to Vietnam on his own?'

'Yeah.'

The sisters could sense the smile in her voice when they called back half an hour later.

'The answer is yes. Billy Patten did visit Vietnam.'

She gave them the month and the year. Beth whooped and immediately looked contrite when a police officer came running.

She made an *It's alright* gesture, and he disappeared.

'That month. The timing,' Meghan mused when the call ended.

'I know.' Beth was bouncing in her chair in excitement. 'It was before he bought the mine. You think he came here to get the two mil?'

'An Khoi?' Meghan called out.

The police officer appeared in the doorway instantly.

'How long do your flight records go back?'

'Why, ma'am?'

He shook his head when she explained. 'Not that far back, ma'am. What about at your end?'

'We're checking.' Meghan looked over at Beth, who was working on a screen.

'Nope, Werner says tough luck.' The younger sister was crestfallen.

'Werner?' An Khoi asked, puzzled. 'Who is that?'

'A…friend,' Meghan replied. 'Even if we had records, it would be difficult to find out who Patten met all those years back.'

'Yeah. Which means we've got to uncover Dang.'

They returned to Sa Dec the next day. This time they made no prior appointment, and took Hy Phuong with them.

They insisted that the police officer dress in plain clothes. 'Cham shouldn't know you're a police officer. You're our translator. That's all he should know.'

Phuong drove them in her own car, a black Toyota, and they reached Sa Dec just after noon.

Cham wasn't home when they arrived. His wife said he was at the fields.

The police officer took the car as far as it could go, and they then trekked to the lush, water-soaked paddy farms.

An expanse of green greeted them when they came to the outskirts of the farmland.

Cham was easy to spot among the several people in the fields. He was alone in his acre, wearing a straw hat as he inspected his rice.

He straightened when Phuong called him. His wizened face broke in a grin when he recognized the sisters.

He might have refused to answer their questions the other day, but that didn't mean he wasn't happy to see them.

He made his way to them and dried himself with a towel that was draped over his shoulder.

'You want to buy his field?' Phuong translated for them.

'We wouldn't know what to do with it,' Beth chortled. 'Ask him about Dang,' she instructed the Vietnamese officer. 'Tell him the police aren't involved. It's just between him and us. We won't tell anyone.'

Cham shouted at another farmer and pointed at a buffalo that was heading to his field.

The farmer acknowledged him and directed the animal away.

'Dang bad,' Cham said in broken English. 'Very bad.'

*Vietnam, 1967–1975*

Luc Cham looked forward to his meetings with Billy, Leroy, and Pete.

He and his platoon went on missions along with American soldiers, and he had developed a fondness for these three.

Leroy and Pete, they were always cracking jokes. Making fun. They knew Cham didn't understand their language, but nevertheless, they tried to include him.

That effort warmed Cham. Sure, he could communicate with the Americans with a few universal words. Everyone understood *VC*, *Charlie*, *enemy*, and such words.

He brought them hot tea in his battered flask whenever he met them. They gave him American cigarettes in return.

Amidst the war, the killing around them, there were a few pleasures, such as puffing away on tobacco.

There were times when Cham went with his unit, no Americans with them. They prowled the jungles and the villages, seeking Charlie, and searching for tunnels.

After one such mission, he was on sentry duty at night while his fellow soldiers slept.

They were close to the banks of the Saigon River, bedded down in the forest.

The SVA soldiers slept either on the ground or on the ragged backpacks they carried. Mosquitos bit at them and sucked on their blood, but most of them didn't notice.

Cham was awake. He paced occasionally to keep himself awake. He prowled in the shadows, knowing that movement was a giveaway and hence keeping close to the trunks of trees.

Sometime in the night, nature's urge came to him.

He went a hundred yards deeper inside the forest and relieved himself against a bush, careful not to make any noise.

He was zipping himself up when he heard whispering.

He cocked his head. This late at night, whispering and stealthy movement could only be the enemy. There were no friendlies near them.

He dropped to the ground and belly-crawled inch by inch in the direction of the sounds.

He parted branches and leaves and reached for the prized possession hanging around his neck.

It was a pair of night vision goggles, NVGs, that Templeman had given him. Cham was the only SVA soldier in his unit to have an American-made pair.

He brought them to his eyes and adjusted them slowly. He stilled when he saw the VC soldier. Charlie was about a hundred and fifty yards away.

Even through the scope, Cham could recognize his uniform

and the AK-47 slung over his soldier.

The VC was talking to someone who was hidden behind a tree. Gesticulating.

Cham slithered forward an inch and brought his rifle around. If there was one VC soldier, there would be others.

He would take his shot, and that would also rouse his men.

He sighted Charlie, flicking his eyes from the binos to his rifle, until he had memorized the VC's location.

He was depressing the trigger for an easy shot when the conversation grew louder and he heard an English word.

Cham frowned. He let go of his rifle and used his binos.

He gasped when he saw the second man step into view.

*Billy Patten!*

Cham didn't believe his eyes for a moment. He looked away for a moment and then peered through the NVGs.

Yes, there was no doubt. Those eyebrows. That nose. That was Billy Patten.

But since when did Billy speak Vietnamese?

No, he didn't. After several moments, Cham noticed that Billy was speaking slowly, repeating himself several times.

He was speaking in English, and Charlie was replying back in the same language.

Their conversation had dropped and Cham couldn't overhear it anymore.

Cham thought furiously. He couldn't shoot the VC while Billy was there. But why was the American soldier talking to the enemy?

Maybe Billy was cultivating a snitch? Yes, that seemed likely.

Satisfied with his reasoning, Cham watched, memorizing every detail about the enemy soldier. The way he talked, his posture, the roundness of his shaven head, the shape of his glasses.

After a long while, Billy handed several folded bills of currency to Charlie.

That confirmed the meeting for Cham. Charlie was surely a VC informer that Billy was talking to.

Cham's suspicions didn't leave him entirely.

He observed Billy Patten for the next few days as they went on missions. The American soldier seemed to be his normal self.

Cham thought of asking him, but he and Billy weren't that close.

He considered going to Leroy or Pete, and there was one moment when the three were smoking in silence. It was ideal for asking them, but Cham's nerve failed him, and it never returned.

As time passed, that night faded from his memory. However, he never forgot that VC soldier's face.

The war continued and then slowed to a stuttering stop. The American soldiers started returning to their home country.

Cham had an emotional parting with Leroy and Pete. They were crying unashamedly, grown men bawling their hearts out, knowing they were lucky to be alive. Not knowing why they had fought in the first place.

And then Cham was sent to re-education camp by the North Vietnamese, who were now establishing their communist government over the unified Vietnam.

The camps were nothing but prisons where the SVA soldiers and prisoners of war were indoctrinated in the ways of the new government and in communist principles.

Cham survived by taking the path of least resistance. He readily embraced all that was taught. Protesting or going against the victors was futile, and besides, he had a wife back home.

Cham was released after three years, and as he made his way out of the camp to a life of freedom, he spotted a man talking to a camp official.

Freedom was in his grasp, his wife awaited him outside the camp's office, but Cham lingered.

He recognized the man talking to the officer. The man had hardly aged.

He was bald, wearing glasses, and despite the passage of time, Cham remembered him.

It was the same VC soldier he had spotted with Billy, in the jungle near the Saigon River.

That soldier's face was burned into his mind.

Cham drifted closer to them, trying to overhear their conversation.

He didn't catch anything, except for a name that he never forgot.

The camp's employee referred to the former VC soldier by one name.

Chieu Ton Dang.

# Chapter 27

*Present Day*

'NVA soldier?' Beth asked incredulously.

Cham nodded his head, understanding her question.

'North Vietnamese, not South Vietnamese?'

Cham did the vigorous head thing again.

Beth exchanged a swift glance with her sister. They had been on the wrong track all along. They had been hunting for Dang in the wrong army.

'That was a long time ago. That man could have been anyone,' she told Phuong, who translated rapidly to Cham.

The elderly man shook his head and gesticulated as he spoke.

'He says he has a good memory. He can remember faces. He says there is a mole on your sister's neck. He saw it just once, for a few seconds, the first time he met you.'

Beth's eyes widened when Meghan pulled aside the neck of her tee and revealed the tiny skin disfiguration.

She clicked her teeth together and stopped gawking when Meghan kicked her leg.

'That… is incredible,' she exclaimed and was rewarded with Cham's gap-toothed grin.

'How does he know Dang is bad, though?'

'He made discreet inquiries about the man. He asked people he trusted. They told him Dang was a businessman. Export and import.

'Cham was ready to leave it at that, but then he reunited with some men from his former unit. They went drinking in HCMC. One of those soldiers told him about an NVA man who used to run a smuggling business during the war. He described the man, and that description fit Dang.

'Cham didn't believe him. But he became curious. He asked more people. He asked people in the underground.'

'Underground? You mean underworld?' Beth questioned her.

Phuong nodded. 'Yes. Criminals. Cham beat up one man, a street pusher, who confessed.'

'Confessed to what?'

'That Dang was a drug runner.'

Cham spoke urgently when he saw the disbelieving look on the sisters' faces.

'He knows what you are thinking. That in those days, during the war, many soldiers used drugs of one kind or another. There was a lot of smuggling.

'He says Dang started off like that, then became big. Now he's one of the largest dealers in narcotics.'

The farmer held his hands wide.

'The largest,' Phuong corrected herself.

'And Cham found this out just by asking people?'

'By asking the right people. And by becoming a mule. He took a year off from his fields after the war. He went to

Laos, where the poppy farms were. Became a mule. Brought it into the country. Joined Dang's gang. Saw him a few times at his warehouses, as he supervised the loading of the drugs. He learned how the drugs are smuggled into our country. How they are distributed.'

'They took him into the gang just like that?'

Phuong translated the question and got a lengthy answer.

'No. They checked him. His background. He told them he had lost everything in the war. That was easy, because it was true. His fields weren't of much value. He had only his wife. No job, no regular income. They didn't believe him at first. They tortured him—'

'Tortured him? Why?' Beth went pale.

'To check if he was from the police.'

'When was this?' The younger twin swallowed. 'When did he take that year off?'

Cham counted on his fingers when Phuong turned to him.

'In 1980.'

'If he knew all this, why didn't he go to the police?'

Cham removed the shirt he wore and presented his back to them.

Beth bit her lips to stop from gasping when she saw the pockmarks and long stripe-like scars on his body.

She recognized them. Cigarette and red-hot poker burns.

'Those are not from the war. They are not the marks Dang's gang made. The police arrested him, they were worse than those gangsters. Cham had taken notes. Descriptions. He had written everything down. The police burned those in front of his very eyes,' Phuong said softly.

'Why didn't they kill him?'

'They threatened his wife. That was better than killing him.'

'Why did Cham go to all that trouble? Why didn't he just get on with his life?'

The farmer looked into the distance, and then at the buffalo that was trudging slowly towards his field.

'He did it for that animal,' Phuong translated, a bemused expression on her face.

The sisters caught on immediately, however.

'He did it for his country,' Beth murmured, at which the old man nodded in understanding.

'He says he didn't survive the war just to see another enemy. Drugs.'

'What if he had died? His wife would have been alone.'

Cham cackled, slapping his thigh.

'He died a thousand times during the war. If he had died in Laos, it wouldn't have been a big deal. His wife was alone during the war. She would have managed if he had died.'

The Vietnamese man smacked his palm against his forehead suddenly and gesticulated excitedly.

'What's he saying?'

Phuong turned to them, her eyes alight. 'He says he has a copy at home.'

'Copy of what?'

'The notes he took. Once he was released by the police, he wrote everything down again. All that he remembered. Kept them safe. They are not as detailed as the original, but he can show them to us.'

Kirilov watched them from his car, his binos to his eyes.

He was behind a bus stop, on a road that bisected fields to the left and the right. Cham's farms were to his right.

In front of him was a broken-down bus that gave him

cover. His windows were mirrored on the outside, and his windshield was dark. No one from the outside could make him out.

Kirilov could read lips. It was one among his many skills that made him stand out, made him one of the deadliest hunters in his world.

He didn't watch Cham; he observed the translator and wondered idly if he had to kill her.

Killing police, even in an emerging country like Vietnam, was never a good thing.

He shelved the half-formed idea and concentrated on the conversation.

He kept the binos down when his watchees walked to the road, toward the translator's vehicle.

He made a call as the Toyota headed towards town, where Cham's residence was.

'Dang is a drug dealer, a big-time criminal,' he told Gorbunov when his boss took his call.

'I can't find any references to such a man,' the Mafia boss responded after a while.

'Are you on your computer?'

'*Da*.'

The two men fell silent, considering the implications.

'He has changed his name,' Gorbunov concluded. He didn't ask if Kirilov was sure, if his killer's information was right. His man was never wrong.

'*Da*,' Kirilov agreed and awaited instructions.

'Did they find anything about Cole Patten?'

'No. They seem to have reached a dead end.'

'Good. This Dang… you remember that one time we tried to get into Vietnam?'

'*Da*. We failed. We lost product, money, and men.'

'Dang—if he is as big as that man is saying, he could be our way back in.'

'By partnering?'

'No,' Gorbunov scoffed, and his next words brought a smile to Kirilov's face.

'By killing him, and taking over his operations.'

Zeb was dressed like a farmer, in a loose pair of trousers and a white shirt, a large Vietnamese hat on his head.

He was sitting next to a bunch of elderly men under a tree and made as if he was talking to them.

He gestured helplessly whenever one of them fired a remark at him and after a while they gave up. The Westerner didn't seem to have any manners. He didn't respond to them. Talking to one another was a better use of their time.

Zeb had Kirilov's vehicle in his sight, but he couldn't see what the Russian was up to.

However, he could make a good guess.

Far behind, he could make out a Jeep with shaded windows.

Bwana and Roger. With those two close, the twins were safe. He could pour all his attention on the Russian.

In less than twenty-four hours, he would regret that he hadn't been closer to Kirilov.

'There's a lot of detail in these,' Phuong said after skimming through the old papers that Cham brought out.

There were about twenty sheets, tied together with a thread, spidery handwriting running across them. There were dates, places, and people's names. That was about all the sisters gathered before handing them to the police officer.

Cham nodded in satisfaction as Phuong broke down the salient points of his records for the Petersens.

He had folded the papers and put them in a tin box and had buried that underneath the front step of his house. It was a simple enough hiding place that it wouldn't stand up to a rigorous search. However, no one had bothered to search his home.

'He has drug-smuggling routes. Locations and dates where he saw Dang. Various key people in his gang. The date the police arrested him. Names of the police officers who tortured him. We should turn this over to An Khoi.'

'We will,' Meghan asserted. 'Ask him if Billy Patten told him anything of his sons.'

Cham looked puzzled and then shook his head.

'No. He had no contact with Billy after the war. He knew about his sons through Pete Garrett, but nothing more. Should I tell him about the accident?'

'Yeah.'

Cham looked troubled when Phuong told him about the events of the past. He stroked his chin and then uttered a few words.

'If there was anyone in Vietnam who knew what happened to Billy Patten, it would be Dang.'

# Chapter 28

Kirilov waited until the Petersens left with their police escort.

He waited for the evening to turn dark and for the lights to come in the village. He was patient. The time had to be right for what he was going to do.

Mothers stood in doorways and called their children who were playing in the streets. It was dinnertime.

In the darkness, hidden in the shadow of an abandoned house, the Russian could smell cooking in the air. Rice, meat, fish from some houses.

He had a keen nose and could distinguish flavors as the breeze wafted in his direction.

He was motionless, as still as the walls of the house. His companion, for he wasn't alone, was more restless. However, the man didn't make much movement, not after the killer had narrowed his eyes in his direction. Not many people disobeyed that look, not even those who didn't know Kirilov.

Lights in the various homes in Sa Dec started turning off as the residents went to bed.

Cham came out of his house one last time and gossiped idly with his friends, all of his age. Someone guffawed and slapped Cham on the back. Cham grinned, shook a finger in admonishment, and went inside his home.

The lights turned off, but still, Kirilov didn't move.

It became midnight, and then one am, and only then did the Russian move.

He beckoned to the man beside him, and the two went silently to Cham's house.

They scaled its wall and went to the rear. Kirilov opened a kitchen window and made his man climb inside first.

Then he followed, and Cham's nightmare began.

Kirilov left two hours later, leaving behind two physical and emotional wrecks, Cham and his wife.

Kirilov could inflict pain in thousands of ways. He could make his victims pray for death.

The farmer and his wife had begged for death. They had pleaded to be spared, but those pleas fell on deaf ears.

Kirilov hadn't stopped until he believed their stories, translated by the Vietnamese gangbanger who was with him.

When he left, it was with a chilling warning.

If Cham and his wife told anyone of what had transpired… they wouldn't die, he reassured them.

They would face a worse fate.

Kirilov and his hood went out of the village as silently as they had arrived.

They went to their vehicle, parked on the outskirts of the village, and set off with dimmed lights.

The Russian made the hood stop the vehicle five miles later.

'Let's relieve ourselves,' he told the Vietnamese. 'It will be a long drive.'

The gangbanger agreed and followed him to the edge of the road where the fields began.

Kirilov snapped his neck, taking care that no urine splashed on his legs, and flung the body into the paddy farms.

There was nothing to link him to the thug. The police would assume it was a gang war killing.

He gave no more thought to Cham, his wife, or the dead hood.

He had accomplished his goal, finding out exactly what the farmer had revealed to the sisters.

He rolled the window down to let the night air in as he drove steadily back.

Zeb had been tricked by a deceptively simple maneuver by Kirilov.

The Russian had switched cars at a crowded intersection where several vehicles had stopped.

He had emerged from his vehicle to investigate the holdup and had returned several minutes later.

It was only when they were at the edge of Ho Chi Minh City that Zeb had realized that the driver wasn't Kirilov. He'd never gotten a good look at the returning driver. He turned out to be someone who looked like the Russian.

He cursed himself for falling for the switch.

He checked his screen. The sisters and Bwana and Roger were back in HCMC.

He turned back at the next opportunity and accelerated towards Sa Dec.

There was only one reason Kirilov would have switched cars.

It wasn't because he believed Zeb was following him.

Neither Cham nor his wife wailed loudly. They sobbed quietly, leaning on each other's shoulders for support.

After a while, Cham got to his feet and hobbled towards the kitchen.

He could walk, even though it felt like his body was on fire.

Their torturer had not left many marks on him or his wife. There were a few bruises, but no cuts, no wounds, no bleeding.

Their interrogator had worked on their nerve and pressure points, in a way that reminded the farmer of the sadistic NVA soldiers.

His wife cried louder when he brought her a glass of water from the kitchen.

She cursed the day he had met the American sisters. She swore at him and warned him to stay away from them.

Cham had his fields. He had a good life. Wasn't that enough for him? Why did he have to revisit the past? Why did he have to get involved?

The old man didn't reply. He was shamefaced, tears trickling down his cheeks.

Neither he nor his wife noticed the shadow in the adjoining room, listening.

Zeb didn't understand the language; however, he didn't need to.

The tone, the manner of the couple's speaking, the glimpses he caught of them, told him volumes.

His face was set when he returned to his vehicle.

He looked at the pale moon in the sky once and made a vow.

There would be one less Russian walking the earth. Soon. Very soon.

The sisters left Sa Dec believing Cham, but not to the extent that they ignored their investigative instincts.

It was Meghan who hadn't fully bought into his story. It wasn't that she disbelieved him. However, his report of joining Dang's gang and extracting information seemed a little too easy to her cynical mind.

'It was a different time. These days, any gang in any part of the world wouldn't just take on new members. They would vet them. Besides, he did get tortured,' Beth argued in his defense. 'You've seen his notes. You're disputing them? Why would he manufacture them?'

'Yeah, that's got me stumped,' Meghan acknowledged, her face troubled. She had grown to like Cham and wanted desperately to think he was telling the truth.

'Records of his arrests.' Her sister snapped her fingers, and Meghan's face lightened.

She knew what Beth was referring to. Communist states loved records. They would detail every little event or incident that their citizens had been involved in.

There would be an archive somewhere of Cham's arrests. The police would have created a fictitious story, but he would be there in the system.

They got Phuong not to reveal a word to An Khoi until they had verified the farmer's account. Not even the fact that Dang was a VC soldier.

They searched the police database for Dangs in the NVA. Such records were less extensive, and when the police officer made some calls, they found out the reason.

The North Vietnamese had been the victorious side in the war and had listed every enemy soldier. They hadn't been so meticulous about their own people.

They went about verifying the new Dangs in the same manner and hit some of the same bottlenecks.

Very few were contactable. Some had died, others had moved to remote areas. Of the handful they spoke to, a couple spoke only when Phuong had to make threats.

'Get your team to contact and verify as many of the Dangs as they can,' Beth instructed their police liaison, who nodded and went out to relay her commands.

When she returned, they switched the focus to verifying Cham's account.

They persuaded her to dig into HCMC's computer systems and, when nothing turned up, asked her to check out where the old records were kept.

They were housed in a government building downtown, Phuong discovered. An office that maintained historical records of all kinds, including police cases.

She had to get An Khoi's authorization for a visit, and when Beth asked her to fake it, 'You'll get me suspended,' was her response.

'We'll make sure you get a promotion,' the American retorted, and that was enough.

The building's security consisted of a few sleepy guards and a portly clerk who made them sign their entry and the reasons for their visit.

Phuong scrawled illegible names and put on her sternest look. She threatened the official, saying he would be cleaning toilets in the remotest part of the country if he disclosed their visit to anyone.

She was investigating corrupt government officials. It was a joint investigation along with the FBI. She pointed to the sisters. Did the clerk really want to be the person who impeded such an operation?

The clerk didn't. He hurriedly led them to a basement and pointed them to rows of shelves.

'They are sorted by department, year, and month. HCMC police records will be in the last rows,' he declared and sped away to the sanctuary of his desk.

It was evening—by then their hands were coated with black ink, and cobwebs had stuck to their hair—when Phuong sighed happily.

She held up a brown folder. 'Cham was right.'

Conspiring against the country was the main reason Cham had been arrested. Making false allegations about other respected citizens was one of the many other accusations made against his name.

The documents noted that Cham had been *convinced* to see the error of his ways. He was a low-level farmer. He didn't need to be prosecuted. He had been urged to lead an illustrious life serving his country.

The police had watched him for several months thereafter, and then the report ended. Evidently Cham had proved to be a model citizen.

The date of the arrest matched Cham's notes.

'Doubting him still?' Beth challenged her sister.

'No,' Meghan replied and mentally apologized to the farmer.

'The problem is,' Beth said, folding her hands and leaning against a rack, 'this gets us no closer to identifying or locating Dang.'

'Yeah, but I know what might.'

'What?'

'We've been going about this the wrong way. We should check out who the current drug barons are. See if they bear any resemblance to Dang.'

# Chapter 29

'You didn't trust me?' An Khoi looked disturbed when they presented the documents to him the next day. 'You didn't come to me in the first place? That Dang was VC is a big development.'

In the span of one day, the search for the NVA soldier had stalled. Phuong's officers had made no progress. The soldiers on their list were either deceased or untraceable.

'We still aren't sure where you stand,' Beth told him frankly, looking at him unflinchingly. 'Not just you, but everyone. Except Colonel General Lanh. We've worked with him before. We know about him. Everyone else in the HCMC police is new to us. Those arrest records show Dang has connections in the police. There's no other reason why Cham would have been arrested and tortured.'

'His contacts would have widened as his business grew,' Meghan added.

'I understand,' An Khoi said stiffly. 'Yet you trusted Phuong.'

The female officer fidgeted, wishing to be anywhere else but in the company of her superior officer.

'She's too young and too junior for Dang to have reached her.'

'He would have no use for her, you mean.'

'Exactly.'

'An Khoi, do you think we would have come to you if we genuinely thought you were on Dang's payroll?'

'Yes, I get that,' he acknowledged and started speed-reading the papers.

He rose abruptly when he'd read the first few and beckoned them to their office. He shut the door once they were inside, his face pale.

'Phuong translated these for you?'

'Yeah, the relevant parts,' Meghan replied, mystified. 'You were right to be suspicious. These are so detailed that if the police didn't act then, I can't see how they would act now.'

He paced the office, thinking furiously, and then turned to Phuong.

'Has he named any officers in the rest of those sheets?'

'Yes, sir. Those who arrested him and tortured him. There are ten names. All of them have retired. But they were high-ranking, in their last positions.'

She rattled off a few names and titles, and An Khoi grew more troubled.

'Those are at the very top of the police,' he explained to the sisters. 'Just because they are retired doesn't mean anything.'

'They would have connections. Or their replacements could be just as corrupt,' Meghan guessed.

The officer nodded and looked questioningly at her when she took Cham's records back, folded them and stuffed them in her bag.

'We can't act on them,' she said, answering his look. 'Let's see where we get with our premise. Start with your current crop of criminals and work back from there.'

Coming up with a list of drug barons wasn't difficult. An Khoi and Phuong produced ten files, men who were suspected of large-scale drug running.

It was equally easy to cross off all those who didn't fit Dang's description.

Beth's face was glum when they tossed all the files away.

Not one of the men fit Dang's description, or even bore such a name.

'There are no others?' she asked the police.

'No. This isn't a large country. We know of every criminal who is out there. Every person who runs an enterprise this big.'

'And they're still at large because you have no proof.'

'Or they have contacts,' An Khoi answered without irony.

Beth swore softly and kicked out at a chair. She leaped forward to grab it before it toppled.

'Something funny?' she snarled when her sister chuckled.

'Yeah. You're missing the obvious.'

Beth righted her seat, taking her time. 'Of course! Dang changed his name—and his face, too. Plastic surgery.'

'Yeah.'

'In that case, there'll be some of these men who are similar in build to him.' Beth pounced on the files, riffled through them quickly, and then stopped in disgust. 'All of them! They're all short and clean-shaven. About the same age Dang would be.'

She looked up and flushed when she saw her sister was still smirking.

'What? What am I missing?'

'It's simple. We get Dang to come to us.'

*Vietnam, 1967, to USA, Postwar Years*

Billy Patten met Dang the day of their rendezvous.

He was careful. Although the two men had conversed the previous day, the other man was still a NVA soldier. He was the enemy.

He reached their meeting place early and lay hidden, in wait, his rifle ready.

He heard Dang's rustling before he saw him.

The soldier's glasses caught a glimmer of light, and then his head emerged from behind a tree and vanished just as quickly.

Billy waited. He had to confirm there was no trap.

Fifteen minutes passed. No other soldiers appeared. Seven thirty pm.

'Billy?' Dang called out softly.

'I'm here,' he answered after a while. 'Throw your rifle away and step out.'

'You throw rifle first.'

'Not happening, dude. I've got your money, remember?'

A pause, and then an AK-47 crashed to the ground.

The NVA soldier stepped out, his eyes swiveling behind his glasses as he tried to spot Billy.

'I'm here.' The American came from behind him and laughed quietly when Dang jumped. 'I could have taken you. But that isn't why I came.'

'What you have in mind?' the enemy soldier asked in broken English.

'What I told you yesterday. A partnership.'

It was an uneasy alliance at the beginning. Neither man

trusted the other. Each one went to a meeting fully expecting an ambush.

However, the lure of money was too strong to resist, and over time, their suspicions disappeared.

Billy gave Dang advance information on the American bombing runs and village raids. That gave the NVA man sufficient time to move his stashes of drugs and money.

He directed Dang to new customers, soldiers on his side who he knew were looking for new highs and addictions.

He had some money squirreled away that not even Rachel knew of.

The day he brought out his own bills, several months later, was the day all mistrust disappeared. Dang regarded him in a new light, and Billy knew the last hurdle had been cleared.

He didn't return the money he had stolen, however. 'I'll manage it. You come to me, I'll give you what you need. It'll be safer where I'm keeping it,' he insisted.

'You don't trust me?'

'After all we've been through? Yes, I do. This isn't about trust. It's about financial management.'

He taught the NVA man English, how to comport himself, and saw Dang change in front of his eyes.

'You get the H from Laos, don't you?' he asked one evening as they sat sharing a cigar.

'It comes from there. But I get it from a supplier in Saigon.'

'How about going to the source? To Laos? To the fields?'

'Will require time.' Dang glanced sideways at him. 'And money.'

'Time?' Billy snorted. 'This war is going nowhere. We have time. Funds too.'

Storing bills was becoming one of their biggest challenges.

New customers, American soldiers who had a thirst for drugs and a seemingly endless supply of money, had fueled their growth.

Billy dug holes around his camp, near outhouses and distant parts, and buried bundles in them. He kept records, and each month, Dang and he ran through the accounts.

They started sourcing the heroin from Laos, and that increased their profits. There were risks. They lost a supply in one bombing run, and in another incident, a Huey ripped at a hut where Dang had hidden several sacks of H.

'That's the price we pay.' Bill shrugged when they totaled up their losses. 'We're still ahead. By miles.'

There were unwritten rules to their deal. By day, Billy still went down the tunnels. He killed NVA soldiers where he found them. Dang attacked American soldiers whenever he could.

The two never fired on each other's units, however, if possible. And never at each other.

The war was grinding to an end. They could feel it. Back home in the US, Americans were deeply dissatisfied with their involvement in Vietnam. Politicians and presidents wanted to end the war.

They didn't discuss politics, however. They were businessmen caught in a war. That's how they saw themselves.

Dang broached the topic one evening a year later. 'What happens when you go back?'

'Nothing changes,' Billy assured him. 'I'll be your partner over there. We can expand in America. I can raise funds. Think of what we can do with more money.'

'I want to come to America.'

# Chapter 30

'You?' Billy looked at him, astonished. 'Why?'

'You said it yourself. We can expand there. Both of us will work better together.'

Billy nodded without answering. This was a wrinkle he hadn't thought of.

'You don't like?'

'I do like.' He grinned and slapped his partner's shoulder. 'Let me go back first. See how it works. Papers and that kind of stuff. It won't be easy.'

'You trust me with business when you are gone?' Dang asked him slyly.

'You trust me with money?' Billy guffawed.

They had worked out their roles early on. Billy was the sales and money man. He was better at accounting. He didn't get into selling because the risk would have been too great.

Dang looked after the operations. The sourcing, the distribution. He knew the local language and the people. It was his strength.

Their parting wasn't emotional.

They met the night before and went through the accounts. Their smuggling business had generated close to a million dollars in the two years they had been working together.

'Buy a house,' Billy told him. 'Establish a front.'

'Front?'

'Some business that makes you look legal.'

'Ah.'

He circled a figure. 'One hundred thousand dollars. Enough to buy a house? And start a business? Like a restaurant?'

Dang calculated rapidly. 'Yes. More than sufficient.'

'Get phones. We will establish a routine for talking.'

'What about all the money? Where will it be?'

Billy smiled wolfishly. 'I've already made arrangements. A joint account. Both our signatures needed to operate it.'

During one of his visits to Saigon, he had opened an account. The bank manager, on seeing the wad of bills he had produced, had been very cooperative.

Yes, Billy could add another name to the account, he beamed. Yes, that could be a Vietnamese name as well.

Regulations? What were those? He had given a knowing smile as he opened the envelope Billy passed him and slid it inside his breast pocket.

'It is legal?' Dang looked at him, surprised.

'Yes. I bribed them. After what we've done, now you're worrying about legality?'

The two shared a laugh.

'This will work?' Dang asked him uncertainly as the American rose to leave.

Billy Patten, the salesman, flashed his smile.

'Yes, it will.'

And it did.

It wasn't easy.

Billy was treated like a hero on his return. Chisholm arranged a parade for his homecoming, and for several months, he was mobbed wherever he went.

There were war protestors too, people who spat at him. His sister-in-law, Ginny, was one such person. Sure, she was civil to him; in fact, she was polite and treated him with respect. And yet, Billy knew she didn't like him, or trust him. Just like her dad, Rachel's father.

Despite all that, he sneaked out in private whenever he could, making excuses to Rachel, and made calls to Dang.

Once a week. That was their routine. He needed to get away. Be alone. Find himself. That was his story he gave Rachel.

He brushed off Dang whenever his partner brought up the topic of his coming to America. 'The timing isn't right. You just wouldn't get a visa. There's a lot of anger and hatred here.'

He got their bank account transferred to an American bank. Bribed more managers and got Dang listed as a joint holder.

He went to Minneapolis, to find himself, and looked up a lawyer and an accountant.

They helped him incorporate a company whose business was to import Vietnamese art and export American luxury goods to that country.

That would be his and Dang's front.

The accountant rolled up their bank account under this umbrella.

Dang was ecstatic. He was now a part owner in an American business.

'Like I told you, podner,' Billy said, putting on a mock-Western accent when next they spoke, 'you leave the management to me. Grow your end of the business and I'll take care of everything else.'

'My coming to America…'

'That will happen too.'

Billy felt adrift, however. He was maintaining a façade, of the returned war veteran. The surviving Tunnel Rat. A man who didn't have much more to him than his Army pension. Who was deeply in love with his wife, Rachel, who was now pregnant.

Only when he was alone, did the mask drop.

He missed the action. The danger. He missed the illicitness of his meetings with Dang.

His partner seemed to have coped better. *But then, he's still running the main part of the business.*

Pete and Leroy visited him. Billy laughed and drank with them, and toasted lost friends. But deep inside, he knew he was no longer like them.

He thought both his friends suspected something was different, but neither brought it up.

And then he read about the failing mine in Chisholm.

It was on the market for five million dollars. A cheap price, he found out after extensive research. The owners were desperate for cash and had lowered their price.

However, there weren't many takers even at that price.

'What do you know about mining, Billy?' Rachel asked him.

'Nothing.' He gave her the winsome smile that had won her over. 'But what did I know of fighting? Or of tunnels?'

'That's a lot of money, honey. We don't have anything close to it. We just have your pension and my teacher's salary.'

'I've thought about that too. I'll approach your father for a loan. I'll go to night school. Learn about business. Study mining. You'll see. It'll work out.'

Rachel's father was a stern-looking individual who smiled only at his wife and daughters. He had grey eyes, and they flashed fire when Billy approached him.

'You want to buy a mine? With my money?' He couldn't keep the derision out of his voice.

'A loan, sir. And I'll build a business out of it.'

'What do you know about steel and mining?'

'Nothing, sir. But I've signed up to go to college. I'm studying everything I need to know about the business.'

'I don't have that kind of money, and even if I did, I wouldn't give it to you.'

'You do, sir,' Billy stated boldly. 'Happy Stay has been posting healthy profits for the last several years. You have virtually no debt. The salaries you pay out are low. Your repeat business is high.'

He rattled off balance sheet figures and knew he had impressed his father-in-law even though the man showed no expression.

'As to why you'll lend me the money, sir, I've taken out a large loan against my house. I've put a down payment on the mine. Just enough to put me in prime position. Rachel's your daughter. You wanted her to have a better life, not be married to me. This mine will give her the good life you wanted for her.'

He didn't need to say any more. If he didn't make good on the loan, he would lose the house. He and Rachel would be homeless.

The father's jaw clenched. 'Let me think about it.'

'I'll give you three million,' was his father-in-law's response a week later. 'If you're so confident about it, you'll raise the rest of it yourself.'

Billy grabbed the offer with both hands.

He was walking through the mine two weeks later when he met Valentine Gorbunov.

'I am Valentine Gorbunov. One of the richest men in Russia. I heard you have right of first refusal on the mine. I have money. We can be partners.'

# Chapter 31

Billy stared at him in amazement.

The Russian had come from behind as Billy was walking to the mine's exit.

He was tall, with thick hair and had a hooked nose.

Billy had to look up to meet his eyes.

'How did you hear about that?' he asked weakly as his brain struggled to catch up and take stock.

'Come. Let's discuss it over a drink.' Gorbunov shepherded him to a waiting Mercedes before Billy could resist.

'There's nothing to discuss,' Billy managed to get out as he sank into the soft leather seats and heaved an inward sigh of relief as the car's aircon cooled him.

'There's always something to discuss,' the Russian stated enigmatically.

The day turned into evening. Alcohol flowed endlessly, waiters snapping to attention whenever Gorbunov raised his head or a hand.

They were at a private table in the most upmarket hotel that Chisholm had to offer.

The Russian was urbane, spoke well, and easily sensed Billy's dark side.

'Some of us have it. The others'—he flicked a careless hand in the direction of other patrons—'they are the sheep. They follow people like us. No?'

'How did you know?'

'I know a lot, Billy. You and I. We are fighters. Survivors. You fought in Vietnam. You were a Tunnel Rat. Here you are, a genuine hero. I fought in the streets of Russia. I am a self-made man, like you. Together we can be great. We can rebuild this mine.'

'Why should I trust you? Believe you? Why should I even deal with you?'

Gorbunov looked around. There was no one within earshot.

'Tell me something, Billy. How did you feel when you killed your first man? Did you puke? Did you have nightmares?'

Billy didn't answer for a moment. He looked into the depths of his glass, at the liquid swirling inside it.

'Nothing. I felt nothing,' he breathed.

'I killed my first man when I was eleven, Billy. Know what I felt? Nothing. Just like you. He was standing in my way. He had to be removed. I did it. Isn't that how you looked at it?'

'That's right,' Billy gasped hoarsely, the image of the NVA soldier, his first kill, coming to his mind.

'*Da*, I thought so.' Gorbunov rose, a king signaling that his court was closed. 'Come tomorrow, Billy. Let us talk about our future. You are drunk now. Tomorrow, you will see I am right.'

Gorbunov spent a week in Chisholm, during which Billy met him each day.

He had discovered a kindred spirit in the Russian. Someone who could easily read him.

Billy knew the Russian had a mafia background. Gorbunov had dropped enough hints about it, which were verified by Billy's research.

'Money is no problem, Billy. One million? Two? Cost is not an issue. I don't think you have all the money, do you? To buy the mine?'

'Why do you say that?'

'If you had, you would have bought it by now.' The Russian winked. 'You are in a dangerous situation, Billy. You have taken that loan out on your house… yeah, I know about that too. You will lose the deposit, the house, everything, if you don't complete the purchase and turn the mine around.

'I can help. We will be equal partners.' He clicked his fingers and an aide sprang forward with a thick folder.

'Those are my accounts. I know you have studied accounting. And mining. And are also learning about business management. Those figures will tell you my story.'

Billy was impressed. Gorbunov had presented him with the five-year balance sheet and profit-and-loss account of Salaluga, the holding company.

There was an auditor's report, from a well-known worldwide firm.

Gorbunov had funds.

'Why do you want this mine?'

'It will be my first steel investment in America. The cornerstone of my empire I will build here. You can be part of that too, or you and I can be partners only in the mine. The choice is yours. Like you, I have studied that mine. I know it has potential. It is bad management that ruined it. Its current owners didn't think big. Don't have imagination.

'You and I, Billy'—he tapped his temple—'we are smart. We can take this business places.'

Billy shook hands with him, signaling a partnership, on Gorbunov's last day in the city.

They worked out the details. How the arrangement would work. How much money each one would pour into the mine. Equal shares, they agreed. Billy would raise two and a half mil, Gorbunov would send an equal amount, and Billy would complete the deal on behalf of the Russian.

*I'll still have enough left over from Rachel's dad's loan to pay back the bank and secure my house.*

And then Dang called and reality struck.

Billy was in Vietnam on the third day after Gorbunov's departure.

'Going to Minneapolis to talk to some investors,' he lied to Rachel.

'What will we do with a steel mine?' Dang looked at him, aghast, when Billy told him everything.

His Vietnamese partner showed few signs of aging. He had a few wrinkles on his face, but that was all.

His body was still lean, wiry, and his glasses were the same.

His restaurant, their restaurant, was doing well. Dang had a nice home, and several mistresses.

After running through the accounts and recounting war stories, Billy had launched into the Chisholm story.

'We're criminals, Dang. We've been smart and lucky, but we can't count on things always being like that. This is our opportunity to start a proper business. A respectable business.'

'What's wrong with a restaurant business? And why steel, Billy?'

Billy spoke long into the night, turning on his charm, launching into the sales pitch he had prepared.

'This will make it easy for you to come to America,' he said, producing his trump card. 'As a shareholder and joint owner of a steel business, you'll get your papers easily.'

'How much?' Dang gave in, and Billy knew he had won.

'Why do you need to route that two mil through me?' Rachel's father frowned when Billy met him on his return.

'Sir, this export-import business,' Billy said, citing the name of the front he had established on his return, 'they'll lend to you. Not to me. They like the idea of the steel mine, its prospects, but lending to you is like a surety.'

'I won't be a guarantor to your business. And I'll need to study their accounts and meet them.'

'No guarantees are needed, sir. I'll arrange the accounts and the call with their director.'

The accounts were good, because they had been designed to look good.

The call with Dang went exactly the way Billy had expected it to, because he had prepped his Vietnamese partner.

In 1970, as Rachel gave birth to twins, Cole and Josh Patten, Billy became the proud owner of Chisholm.

As he became involved in the running of the mine, Billy's relationship with Dang soured.

He had avoided all contact with Valentine Gorbunov after a few heated calls.

He didn't need Gorbunov anymore and had tried explaining

that to the Russian, who hadn't taken it well. He had threatened Billy.

'I survived Vietnam. I can live through whatever you throw at me,' Billy had replied and hung up forever on Gorbunov.

He didn't deliberately ignore Dang. It was just that he no longer felt the urgency of keeping his partner informed about all that was happening in the steel business.

Then there was the small matter that Dang was never a shareholder in the business. Billy had sole authority to act on his partner's behalf and had structured the corporation such that he was the sole owner.

Dang was incensed when he learned about it. He felt cheated.

'You will not get a single dollar from the Vietnamese business,' he screamed from across the ocean.

'I don't need anything from you,' Billy snapped. And he didn't.

'I should have killed you in the tunnels.'

'You're forgetting. It was me who had the drop on you. You're alive because of me.'

'You lied to me about everything.'

'I didn't.'

'You are lying even now,' Dang yelled, and Billy couldn't resist a smile at the image of the small, red-faced man screaming into his phone, cords bulging on his neck.

'If you come to Vietnam again,' Dang said, his voice dropping to an ominous whisper, 'you will never leave.'

# Chapter 32

*Present day*

'How would we get Dang to come to us?' Beth ran her fingers through her hair. 'And, why would he?'

'Because that's what we would do,' Meghan replied patiently. Most times, her sister connected the dots before they were formed. And then there were times like this. 'If we knew someone was investigating us.'

'Oh, you mean that…'

'Yeah, that. Took you all day to figure it out.'

'An Khoi may not go for it. He'll have to get authorization.'

'We won't involve him.'

'What about Farrell and Patten?'

'Yeah, we'll tell them.'

'Tell, not ask?'

'Yes.'

'If the Vietnamese police don't know who Dang is, those babes won't find out either,' Gorbunov told Kirilov.

He had listened in satisfaction when his killer told him

about Cham's interrogation. That his man had destroyed the farmer's life didn't matter. He had liked it even more when he'd learned the Vietnamese gangbanger was now turning into organic compost

That was Kirilov. He left no loose ends.

Still, there were times when his shooter surprised him. Like when he told his boss that he had bugged the Petersens' office.

'The New York one? What good is that when they are in Vietnam?' Gorbunov had harangued him.

'Not that one. I couldn't get close to that. Too much security. The one they have in Ho Chi Minh City. In the police headquarters.'

'You bugged the police offices?' Gorbunov's feet slipped off his desk.

He tried to imagine the logistics involved, the sheer gall, and then gave up. If there was anyone in his outfit who could enter a police building, plant a surveillance device, and walk out unscathed, it was his top shooter.

Kirilov didn't answer. He was like that, too. He didn't like using too many words.

'So, what will they do now?'

'I don't know,' his man answered. 'They moved out of their room. I haven't wired the whole building.'

Gorbunov drummed his fingers on his desk as he thought back to the several sheets he had read on the twins.

Lateral thinking. Imagination. MIT kind of smart. He recalled the criminals and terrorists they had put away.

'They'll dangle some bait. Get this drug dealer to come out of cover.'

'Yes. It's what I would do.'

'And when he does, you will capture him. Squeeze everything out of him.'

'What about those sisters?'

'They are not coming back. You will take care of them. That older one, Meghan, she assaulted me. No one does that to Gorbunov and lives.'

'I thought you deliberately antagonized them.'

'Yes. But I do that to many people. Only these two dared to raise a hand to me.'

The sisters made all the arrangements. They contacted Colonel General Lanh, who didn't ask any questions when they told him what they wanted.

*He must wonder why we didn't ask An Khoi.* 'Your contacts will be senior, sir. That's why we came to you,' Meghan explained after she noted the names the official mentioned.

She twisted around to watch her sister, who was on another phone, speaking intensely, one finger curling through her hair.

'Yes, sir. I'm here. We want to place an ad,' she told the colonel and suppressed an untimely giggle at the silence on the other end.

'They want to run an ad,' Farrell briefed Cole Patten in the latter's office. 'I greenlighted it.'

A fleeting expression crossed the billionaire's face as he heard out his lawyer.

'What? I thought you wanted to find out who you were.'

'I did.' Patten crossed his arms. 'But are you sure an ad is the right way to go? They'll get crank calls. A zillion of them. How will they sift through all those?'

'I think it's a great idea. Someone will know something.

They'll also run another ad, about Dang. As to the crank calls…' Farrell shrugged. 'I'm sure they'll hire people to weed those out.'

'That could be dangerous.'

'I think you'll find the Petersen twins can take care of themselves.'

Farrell was troubled when he left his client's office. He and his firm had been advising Patten and Chisholm for several years, and over time, he had gotten to know his client well.

They weren't friends; they didn't go golfing or fishing or watch ball games together. However, they were reasonably close. Farrell thought he knew his client well, knew everything about him.

And yet…*Why did he cross his arms? That's a defensive posture.*

Beth had arranged for a Vietnamese call center to deal with the incoming flood of calls.

It had been recommended by Lanh for being discreet and competent. The sisters inspected it, met all the agents and got the staff to sign confidentiality agreements, and then went to the newspapers.

The ads ran in ten Vietnamese papers, in both the local language and the English editions.

There were two advertisements. One sought information on the accident involving Billy Patten and his sons. It offered a reward for the correct information.

The twins, knowing that there could be several false calls, had written a verification script for the agents. Each caller had to confirm the exact tunnel that had collapsed.

Since the police had made incorrect information public, only a witness would have the correct details.

There could be police officers who called, in which case An Khoi could check into their story.

The second ad offered no reward. It sought information on a former NVA soldier named Dang, who was also a narcotics smuggler.

The sisters expected the second advertisement to create unease in the underworld as well as amongst certain police ranks.

Turmoil was what they were after. Dang or his emissaries reaching out—that was what they hoped would happen.

Nothing much happened for three days, other than a high volume of incoming calls.

All turned out to be hoax, except one.

A farmer in a village on the banks of the river called.

Bui Khac Tuy correctly identified the location of the accident. However, he quickly dashed their hopes.

He had been working in his fields when he'd heard the rumble of the tunnel collapsing. He had come running to the site and seen the boy at the edge of the hole, heard him crying. He had seen the other farmer rushing in as well and had then retreated.

His paddy had to be harvested, and that was the more pressing concern for him.

The sisters called him back and questioned him at length, but they got no more out of him.

They went out for a run for the fourth day, burning their frustration, turning it into perspiration and panted breaths.

They took a longer route while returning, going through several small alleys, inhaling diesel fumes along with odors of Western and Vietnamese fast food.

It was when they were in the middle of an alley that seemed to be more garbage dump than street, that they spotted the four men.

They came out of a vehicle that blocked their route and waited.

Meghan flicked a rapid glance at her sister and got a waggle of Beth's fingers.

They were armed, ready for anything.

'That ad says you got reward money,' one of the young men, heavyset and larger than the rest, called out in passable English. 'We want that.'

His hand started reaching behind him.

*When the numbers are against you, go for the biggest attackers. That's what Zeb says. People have this thing about size. They think size wins the battle. Put down the big men and chances are, the odds will even.*

Meghan launched herself into the air, left leg crossed, tucked tightly against her thigh, right leg outstretched and perfectly horizontal, upper body leaning back slightly to reduce drag, her green eyes focused only on the speaker.

Then she was on him, kicking him back against the vehicle's hood. She felt one of his ribs break, a scream emerging from his throat. She landed on the windshield, rolling off the vehicle onto her feet, and used her momentum to grab another hood and smash his face against the car.

Two down in less than a minute. Out of the corner of her eye, she caught Beth punching the third assailant.

Someone caught her hair and yanked her back savagely.

Off balance, she thrust her right leg against the vehicle and pushed back with all her strength.

Her attacker was expecting resistance. He wasn't prepared for her full body weight flying back at him.

He gave a startled yelp and fell, with Meghan on top.

An elbow to his nose and a palm slamming into his throat took him out of the fight.

'You alright?' she gasped at her sister.

'Never better.' Beth rolled her shoulders like a boxer and cracked her knuckles. 'That was a half-decent workout.'

She grabbed the large man's hair and pounded his head on the hood, once, twice, and three times, until his face was covered in blood.

'Who sent you?'

'No…one,' the man moaned pitifully. 'Was… our…idea.'

'How did you find us?'

'Call…center…friend…told…us…about…you. Followed …you…in…car.'

Meghan and Beth searched the men quickly. They found wallets and knives. No guns. They broke the blades, flung them away, pocketed the rest of the belongings and resumed their run.

Just another day in the lives of the Petersen twins.

The large man lay moaning, watching them recede into the distance, and only when they turned a corner did he rise.

He swayed on his feet and was readying to yell at his companions when someone grabbed him and flung him against a wall.

He shrieked when a shoulder dislocated and bawled in agony when he slid to the ground.

Two pairs of boots came in his vision.

He lifted his eyes with difficulty and took in the large black man and the slightly shorter blond.

'I'll only ask you once,' Bwana growled. 'Who sent you? Lie, and I'll break your neck.'

Kirilov watched them from the mouth of the alley. He had observed the twins take on the men, dispatch them and resume their run.

He watched the black man question them and dislocate another shoulder.

He approached the four hoods when Bwana and Roger left, and surveyed the broken men before him.

Kirilov too wanted to know who had sent the four thugs. If it was Dang, he would question them aggressively. If it wasn't…well, it never hurt to practice his interrogation techniques.

'Who are *you*?' one man gasped.

The Russian's brows drew together. Surely, they could see it in him, who he was.

'Death,' he replied.

# Chapter 33

The calls on Dang were flaky. They had to investigate each call because there was little by way of verification.

The agents asked the callers how they knew Dang and where they saw him.

Not one was able to offer much information; all seem to be after the reward money.

A few calls took them on trips outside HCMC to check out warehouses.

They went alone, expecting to be ambushed, but found rotting structures and dead rats.

They ran the ads for a second time, on the fourth day. This time they blanketed the Vietnamese newspapers. Each daily in the country carried the two advertisements.

The response was no different.

A full eleven days after the first run of the ads, they gave up.

Beth called their Gulfstream and made arrangements for their return.

They visited An Khoi and Phuong and thanked both of them. They called Colonel General Lanh, who brushed away their appreciation. It was nothing, he said. He would do anything for Zeb or his crew.

They made plans to visit Cham the next day and bid him farewell.

It was evening when the sisters returned to their hotel, after a day of seeing the sights in HCMC.

Beth followed Meghan into her room and tossed her bag onto the bed.

Some sixth sense made them whirl around.

There, coming out of the bathroom and from the closet, were three men.

All three were holding some kind of weapons in their hands.

No time to figure out how they had gotten in. No time even to call out.

Meghan shoved Beth to the floor with her left hand, flinging her to relative safety.

Her right hand flickered in a lightning draw.

Too late.

Blue and white ribbons arced out of the Tasers in the men's hands and landed on their bodies, rendering them helpless.

One of the men plunged syringes into them, and they slipped into darkness.

Meghan kept her eyes closed when she came to, lying still, listening, *feeling*.

She sensed another body close by and opened her eyes a fraction.

Beth was a foot away, both of them on hard ground. Their legs and wrists were tied, their hands behind their backs. Their jackets removed, but they were still in their tees, jeans, and sneakers.

Their shoes had GPS transponders. *But it's not as if any of the crew are around to help us.*

Meghan's head was clear; whatever they had been drugged with hadn't left any lingering effects.

She breathed slowly, without giving away that she was awake.

She smelled earth. Air that didn't seem to have much circulation. She sensed they were in a small room, just the two of them. She couldn't detect the presence of another body. No small movements, no breathing other than Beth's.

She cracked her eyes half-open.

Mud, baked earth stared back at her.

*Mud!*

Her eyes opened in shock and she jerked her head up.

Fluorescent light hanging from a cable off the ceiling. Bare walls and floor. No decoration, no furniture. Just earth, the smell of old air, and their perspiration.

*We're underground.*

Beth sucked in her breath as she moved beside her.

'You think we're where I guess we are?'

'Yeah. In one of the tunnels.'

She rolled upright and gave a shoulder to her sister to lean on and rise.

Beth looked pale, twin spots of color on her cheeks. Her hair mussed, her eyes fierce.

Angry. Furious just like she, at having allowed themselves to be taken so easily. They had walked right into a trap.

Before she could say anything, footsteps sounded.

A man stepped in, and she couldn't control the gasp that escaped her.

'We meet again,' Nang Quy Dang greeted them. 'I am Chieu Ton Dang.'

Six men came behind the Vietnamese man, all armed, all similar in build. Short, clean-shaven, alert, pointing AK-47s in their direction.

One man stepped forward at a nod from Dang and cut their bindings. The sisters were outnumbered, there was no risk of their escaping.

Meghan recognized three of the gunmen immediately. *The same men who snatched us.*

'You—'

'I am the same man you are hunting.' Dang smiled superciliously, feeling pleased with himself.

'All this time—' Meghan struggled to get hold of herself, but the shock was too great.

'I call it hiding in plain sight.' Their captor clapped his hands together, chortling. 'It gave me a lot of pleasure, seeing you flounder. I knew everything from the moment you contacted the police. And all along, I was right there. You even interviewed me.'

'Colonel General Lanh?' Beth guessed. 'He's your man?'

'Not him.' Dang waved dismissively. 'Not any of the men you spoke to. There are others. How do you think the police never had a file on me? Never suspected me? You thought I had plastic surgery, didn't you? There was no need. I changed my name, expanded my art business, put powerful politicians and police officers in my pocket. That was more than enough.'

'But you said you were in the South Vietnamese Army. There are records. We checked you out.'

'All manufactured. All fake!'

It was too much to take in. Meghan looked around them, processing it, trying to stay on top.

The room they were in was small. A couple of exits, one through which Dang and his men had entered, the other behind them.

She had a million questions for the Vietnamese and knew her twin had many too.

*Most can wait. However, there are a few that need to be asked.*

'Why did you break cover now? If you knew all about us, you could see we weren't making progress.'

'Those ads,' he replied. 'I could control a lot. All those who knew me during the war, I either bought them or killed them. But those advertisements…they were a stroke of genius. They posed a risk. There could be someone out there who knew the real me. Someone I had forgotten about. A loose end.'

'So, you *are* a criminal, a drug smuggler?' Beth asked, trying to get a confession from him.

'Baron. Drug baron,' Dang corrected her. He was still wearing that superior expression. He was dressed in a white suit, polished shoes, as if he was holding court in a boardroom. 'Yes, I am that, and more. I am the biggest criminal the Vietnamese do not know of,' he boasted. 'I am involved in every illegal activity in this country.'

*That acknowledgment won't do us any good. We aren't recording it.*

Meghan took in the armed men standing behind the suited men. There were three; the others had circled around and were behind the sisters.

The hoods looked competent. The way they held their weapons and stood loose, yet ready, spoke of experience. She could make out spare mags on their belts, knives on their bodies, and was that a grenade in a pouch?

Yeah, it was. All three carried one.

Patten. Her ears pricked when the name was mentioned.

Beth was speaking, asking the criminal about Billy Patten.

'He betrayed me.' Dang cursed at length in Vietnamese and then switched to English. 'He posed as a friend initially. We became close, and then he turned out to be a snake. I trusted him. We built a big drug operation during the war. I even gave him money to buy that steel mine. And then he showed his true colors.'

'How did you meet him? He was on the opposite side.'

'Not far from here.' The suited man pointed to a wall and smiled unpleasantly when Beth drew a breath. 'Welcome to the undiscovered and unknown part of the Cu Chi tunnels. A passage away is where we met for the first time. He stole my money. That was our first encounter.'

He seemed to be in no hurry. He spread his feet wider, rubbed his hands together and launched into his story.

*I wish we could have recorded this*, Meghan thought dimly as she listened.

Dang's tale was breathtaking. The way Billy and he had come together was audacious. In the middle of one of the most intense wars in American history, the two enemies had come together and collaborated on a criminal empire.

Dang was expansive, knowing he had a captive audience. He told them every detail. How he and Billy Patten had overcome their distrust. How they had built on the small operation he had started.

'No one suspected?' Beth asked in disbelief.

'No. That was the smartest idea Billy came up with. Who would believe that an American soldier and a Charlie were business partners?'

'And you pulled this off during the war? Surely someone could have seen you. Or you could have been killed. The Americans could have bombed your hideouts.'

'They didn't. Billy gave me advance information. And there *was* a witness I knew of. However, I found out about Cham only after the war. The police made sure he kept quiet.'

'He didn't,' Beth retorted.

'Yes, I know that now. But what good did it do you?' he gloated.

'You funded Chisholm?' Meghan asked, still digesting his story.

'We were still partners then. The steel mine was to be our first American investment. A clean business. And then I found out how good Billy was at lying,' Dang replied bitterly. He gave them more details.

'You know why we're here?'

'Yes. I read newspapers. I didn't know English when I first came across Billy. But now'—he gestured at himself, taking pride in his appearance—'I am an international businessman.'

'A common criminal,' Beth spat.

'Not common at all,' he countered. 'You didn't find me despite your investigation.'

Meghan shot a *drop it* look at her sister. 'You know what happened in the tunnels? To Billy and Josh Patten?'

Chieu Ton Dang whirled on his feet instead of answering. 'Follow me,' he ordered over his shoulder.

He led them through a tunnel that had been widened and was well lit. Through another bare room, past an opening, and to a door.

He unlocked it with a security code and couldn't help chuckling when Beth gasped.

'Meth. My newest product.' He gestured at the laboratory in front of them.

Beakers and plastic containers were strewn on metal tables. Cans of chemicals, red phosphorous and kerosene were on the floor. Rubber tubes, iodine bottles and several other containers were scattered around the room.

'All this is underground?' Beth shook her head as if she was in a dream.

'Yes. We made the tunnels bigger, put in lighting, ventilation. This unknown part of the Cu Chi complex is the heart of my operation. Eight miles of secret passages. This is where my products are stored. Where my new meth lab will operate from. It's a new business for us. We are still learning.'

'How long has this been here?'

'Always, during the war and ever since.' He chortled. 'The police took you to the opening of the collapsed tunnel?'

Beth nodded.

He went to a wall and slapped it with a hand.

'That tunnel is next to this. We have several openings throughout the jungle for our business. We patrol it discreetly. We post it as government property. The police, politicians, they know nothing about what happens here. They think some obscure department owns the area. We know who enters the jungle, who leaves. We control everything.'

Meghan went to the wall, ignoring the menacing click of weapons from the guards.

'That's where Billy and Josh died? Behind that wall?'

'Cole Patten.' Dang's spectacles glinted in the light.

'Cole Patten died that day. Josh Patten is alive.'

# Chapter 34

*Vietnam, 1979*

Billy Patten couldn't resist the temptation.

He wrestled with it for months as his boys grew up. Rachel had died during their birth, and for months, life had become dark and bleak for him.

He had hired a nanny to help with raising them, resisting all approaches from her family. He had no time for them once he had repaid her father's loan. He and they were never close, and once she died, there was no longer any reason to maintain contact.

Of course, his in-laws tried to maintain a relationship. Cole and Josh were their grandchildren, after all. They made overtures. They wanted to help in bringing them up. They invited Billy and his sons for Christmas, remembered birthdays. However, those invites and requests dwindled as he ignored them. Then they stopped.

The nanny became like a second mother to the boys, and when they were seven, he succumbed.

He took Josh and Cole to Vietnam.

He was careful. He remembered Chieu Ton Dang's threat and knew the Vietnamese would be a bitter enemy.

He booked several flights as decoys and reserved hotel accommodations in several names.

He prepped the boys, told them about the history of the war, the reasons American soldiers had been there. They asked several questions, which was natural since he had never opened up about those years. They were excited as well.

He made a will and deposited it with Farrell for safekeeping. Cole Patten would inherit Chisholm if anything happened to him, and Josh Patten would get his father-in-law's hotel chain.

Despite the estrangement, Rachel's folks had sworn that everything they had would go to the boys. Billy had initially been thinking of dividing those assets evenly among the two. That was before Chisholm had become such a success. Now, splitting the hotel wasn't needed.

They arrived in Ho Chi Minh City in the summer. It was hot and humid. Billy and the boys enjoyed it. He took them to the tourist spots, reveling in their enjoyment as they took in the city he had previously known as Saigon. Ben Thanh Market, City Hall, Independence Palace, the basilica, he showed them all the places.

The plan was to spend just a week and stay in the urban parts of HCMC, but temptation again got the better part of Billy.

On the penultimate day of their visit, he rented a vehicle and drove the boys out of the city, towards the river.

Towards the tunnels.

He didn't take them to the tourist area of Cu Chi; he detoured and went deeper until the green embraced them and swallowed the sunlight.

Sounds of the city fell away as he drove carefully over nonexistent tracks.

When the vehicle could proceed no more, he jumped off and led them on a hike.

They had water cans and backpacks with food. It was a grand adventure, and he knew what the boys would see would blow their minds.

The tunnel's opening stood in exactly the same spot he remembered. The village he had fled from all those years back was no more. The jungle had conquered the area it had occupied.

He stood in the small clearing, hands on hips, and watched his sons. They looked around, puzzled, and then Josh turned to him.

'Dad, what's here?'

In the distance, they could hear the muted sounds of the river.

'Don't you see it?' he laughed.

They peered here and there, looked under bushes, and then gave up.

He got Josh to step back, leaned down, scraped the dirt away with his hands, and there was the trapdoor.

'This was one of the tunnels I discovered. No one knew of it then. It wasn't used by the Viet Cong. It was empty. It'll give you an idea of what we did.'

*Dang used it, but they don't need to know that.*

He gave them careful instructions, tied a rope around all three of them to link them together, got out flashlights from his backpack, and handed one to each of them.

He then attached a belaying rope to a tree and headed down first, Josh following, and lastly, Cole.

Billy had taken care of his body and had no flab. He could crawl through the tunnel just as he had done during the war. His sons were far smaller and could easily cope.

He pointed out the places where VC would bury traps, and he could sense their excitement.

The tunnel had started crumbling in several places, and when they reached the small room, there were mounds of dirt on the floor, fallen from the ceiling.

Cole kicked one mound, and Billy was suddenly struck by how dangerous, how foolhardy he had been.

*These haven't been maintained. They could collapse.*

He let the boys explore for a while, his eyes searching for the wall with the hidden door.

He went to it, felt the wall, and found the concealed opening.

He had to strain to open the door, and more dirt fell when he wrestled with it.

It gave way suddenly, and he leaned inside.

The hiding place was empty. In place of the sacks were heaps of mud and rodent droppings.

'I knew you couldn't resist coming here.'

Billy froze. He knew that voice well.

He drew back and swung around. Chills raced through him when he spotted Dang.

His former partner was in a pair of khakis and a white shirt. It was muddy in places. He too had crawled through the tunnel.

His right hand held a flashlight, the other was behind his back.

'You thought you could visit secretly and I wouldn't know?'

Dang hadn't changed. The same height, the same weight, the same style of glasses. A few wrinkles, but that was the only difference in his appearance. His English had improved.

The twins looked uncertainly at the stranger and then at their father. They sensed something was off.

'Do they know this was where you betrayed me?'

*This was where I stole your money*. However, Billy didn't correct him.

'Not here, Dang.' He moistened his lips, his heart thudding. This wasn't in the script he had planned, in the visit he had organized. 'We can talk in the city.'

'No more talking, Billy.' Dang shook his head. 'That time has gone.' A fire danced in his eyes, and even over the distance, his hate and rage could be sensed.

'I have waited so long for this, Billy. I can't hold back any longer. You are a traitor. You are a snake—'

'*Stop!*' Billy roared. His boys started. 'I will meet you in HCMC. Anywhere you want. Let's talk then. Not here, not in front of my boys.

'Let's go.' He gestured at them and started hurrying towards the hole.

Dang sprang in front of him, and Billy saw that he was holding a Smith and Wesson in his left hand. 'You are not going anywhere.'

'My boys are here, Dang.' Billy shoved him away roughly and tugged at the rope, jerking Josh and Cole forward.

'You should have thought of that before bringing them here.' The Vietnamese snarled as he got to his feet and blocked their way again. 'Do they know what you did to me? Do they know how evil you are?'

'*Enough!*' Billy snapped and reached out with his free hand to push the man away. He mistimed his action, or perhaps it was Dang who moved. His gesture ended as a blow to the Vietnamese's face.

For a second, Dang stood still, and then he growled and sprang at Billy.

The American went down as his former partner rained blows on his face and chest. Cole and Josh started yelling and screaming, the rope linking them drawing them closer to the fight.

Billy wrestled with his opponent, sweat streaming down his face. 'Behave, Dang. Those are my boys,' he said through gritted teeth and winced when the Vietnamese punched him in the neck.

He swore and swung back, landed a blow on the man's temple.

Dang's finger curled instinctively and his gun went off.

Everyone stopped. Billy snapped a look at his attacker, then at his gun, which was pointing at a wall.

*Didn't hit me*. He started to relax, when the secret room collapsed.

There was no warning. No indication. It could have been because of the reverberations of firing. Or just age and nature taking their toll.

The clay walls fell in a loud slithering sound, raining dust and chunks of mud in the room.

Billy pushed Dang away roughly and got to his feet.

'My God,' he whispered, just as another wall fell.

'*Run!*' he told his sons.

Josh, who was in the front, whirled and raced to the tunnel. The rope around his waist dragged Cole, and then Billy.

But Dang hadn't given up.

He caught Billy by his shoulder and pulled him back. 'Remember what I told you, Billy?' he hissed.

'For Chrissakes, Dang,' Billy yelled as the floor shook, a rumble sounded, and the wall in front of them started cracking.

'No.' The Vietnamese was wild in anger, beyond reasoning.

Billy punched him in the gut and reached feverishly behind him. He grabbed his backpack, brought it forward, and ripped it open even as he took stumbling steps forward.

He drew out his knife. 'Josh,' he shouted hoarsely, tossing it at him. 'Cut yourself free. Then give it to Cole.'

His son was already crouching to crawl inside the exit tunnel. He stopped, turned, grabbed the blade from the floor and sawed desperately at the rope.

The ground shook and the roof started collapsing, slowly at first and then faster as the structure could no longer support it.

Mounds of earth, like rocks, fell. Some of them bounced. Loose dirt poured like rain. It looked and felt like an avalanche of clay.

'Hurry,' Billy urged and looked behind him. Where was Dang?

The Vietnamese was digging through the fallen wall, clawing away at it, at the rear of the room.

*That's where he came from.*

Billy put him out of his mind.

'Cole,' Josh shouted as he freed himself and gave him the knife.

'Go, Go,' Billy told his younger son, snatching the knife from Cole and cutting at the rope holding the two of them.

Perspiration beaded off his nose and fell. The knife was

slippery and didn't grip well, but he persisted, nicking his fingers a few times. His elder son came closer, attempting to help, urgency flooding them.

And then the roof collapsed on top of them. An earthen rock struck Billy on the shoulder and brought him to his knees. Dust choked and blinded him. He coughed, sucking air through his mouth, taking shallow breaths—otherwise, his lungs would be filled with clay.

He lost the knife and searched blindly for it, fear flooding him.

Someone came close to him. Cole. He grabbed his son, hauled himself to his feet, and dragged them forward.

Another mountain of rock fell, blocking their way.

'Dad,' Josh's voice came from afar.

'Josh, run,' Billy shouted as loudly as he could, knowing his voice would never be heard again.

# Chapter 35

*Present Day*

'How did you get away?' Beth was fascinated despite their predicament.

They were in a secret tunnel near Saigon River, captured by Dang and his men. Despite their circumstances, the Vietnamese's story had them spellbound.

'My escape route was behind that first collapse.'

'Let me guess,' Meghan butted in sarcastically, 'you had that strengthened. Your tunnel didn't collapse.'

Dang walked swiftly along the wall of the meth lab and tapped a section of the wall close to the secured entrance.

'My escape route is behind this wall,' he announced proudly. 'Don't use it anymore.'

Beth examined their surroundings carefully. 'This isn't concrete. It's clay. It doesn't look strong.'

The walls and roof were painted white to give the illusion of strength.

'Strong enough for our work. We only store the drugs here. It's our warehouse.'

'You're cooking now.' She pointed to the equipment in the room.

'That's new,' Dang admitted. 'In any case, we don't intend to shoot here.' He sniggered. 'There is a new building we are constructing in the jungle. Everything will be moved there, once it's ready.'

'So, it was Josh all along,' Meghan murmured to herself, still thinking of Billy Patten's last moments.

'Yes.'

'You read the news. What's happening to Cole, no, Josh Patten, and to Chisholm. The allegations against him. The takeover attempt. You could have done something.'

'And expose myself? I am not stupid.'

'You could have tried other means. Sent an anonymous letter.'

'I want nothing to do with any Patten.' Dang compressed his lips. 'What happens to Josh Patten is not my business.'

'You killed his father and brother.' Beth rounded on him.

'I fought with him. I didn't cause the tunnel to collapse. I didn't invite him inside the tunnels. I would have killed Billy Patten. But not there, and not like that.'

Dang was cold, remorseless, as he stared them down.

Meghan's skin prickled at what he left unsaid. Her heart beat faster. Adrenaline surged through her, readying for whatever was in store.

She drifted closer to one of the tables. Fingered its edge, her hand close to a chemical container.

Three men behind them. Dang and three more in front.

*He didn't bring us here just to tell stories.*

'But you,' Dang continued without inflection, 'you will die here. In the tunnels. Deliberately.'

She snapped her head up. 'That would be a mistake. We're Americans. We work for a security consulting company in New York. We have friends. The New York Police Department knows us very well. There will be investigations, relentless ones. You will be found.'

Dang's lips twitched. 'That's what everyone says. All those who are about to die. You really thought I would let you go?'

He removed his spectacles, polished them and drew himself to his full height. 'No one discovered me all these years. Even you. It was I who came to you. You would have returned to America without knowing anything about me.

'And your being American? Your friends? The New York police?' he sneered. 'You know how many American tourists die in Vietnam? How many are kidnapped, raped and murdered? Your death will be an accident. Stupid tourists straying into the jungle. Falling into an undiscovered tunnel.'

His voice didn't change, no expression crossed his face, and yet Meghan spotted the slight shift in his eyes. A signal to the men behind them.

She exploded.

Her left hand grabbed a beaker. Her right grabbed Beth and flung her to the side.

Few people could maintain a continual state of alertness. Not even trained operatives.

Dang's story, his tour of the tunnels, had made his men relax. They had numbers on their side. They had weapons. The sisters were captives in their domain.

Yes, they were watchful, but they had lost the edge.

*I hope I'm right.* One second for Meghan to pivot on her

left foot. In the same move, she flung the beaker at the thug in the middle. A fraction of a second to kick the hood in front of her.

A full second to follow up with a throat punch, disarm him, grab his AK, and shove him in front of her.

She fired a burst into the third man and turned.

Dang stood open-mouthed. His men caught unawares, trying to react. All of them staring in disbelief. One hood screaming, the one at whom she had hurled the chemical. Smell of burning flesh.

Beth no longer on the floor. She had scooted under the table. Was upending it. Cans and chemicals splashing to the floor. Glass all over. Fumes rising. Smell of acid.

Beth pushed the table. Turned it around. Meghan ducked under it, raised her hand and let loose a burst at Dang and his men.

They dove away to safety. Two men hauling Dang away.

Screaming, yelling, and cursing filling the air.

Less than a minute since she had first moved. Luck, and their training, giving them the upper hand.

Something smacked into the table from behind them. A knife.

She rolled on the ground, her AK coming up to cover them.

The guard she had disarmed had risen on his elbow, his hand shaking, something in it. A grenade.

'Incoming,' she screamed. She tossed the rifle to Beth, who fired long bursts at Dang and his men, pinning them down. The rounds didn't seem to hit anyone, but they did what they were designed to do.

Buy them time.

Meghan kicked out with her legs. Pushed back at the table.

Swung it around by sheer momentum, grabbed her sister back. Somehow got the table roughly parallel to the wall. On its side. Its metal surface shielding them from the hoods behind them, and partly from Dang's men.

The grenade didn't explode. Dang was shouting. His men started firing at the table.

'*Stop!*' Dang yelled in English. His men stopped, but it was too late.

Flames burst in the room with a *whump*. They started spreading across the floor, from the back to the front.

Two of Dang's guards threw away their weapons and tried to douse the fire. They grabbed plastic cans of water and emptied them.

However, there was more flammable material than water. More chemicals caught fire and the heat started intensifying.

The hoods at the rear started screaming as their clothing caught fire.

Someone kicked at the locked door. Meghan risked another look.

Two hoods surrounded the door. The ones who had been behind them were patting at one another, trying to smother the flames. Thick smoke in the air, already smothering all of them. Every guard had flung away his AK. Survival was more important than attack.

Dang's face was red. He babbled incomprehensibly as he stood at the wall, fingering it. The same spot he had pointed to, behind which he claimed his tunnel was.

Even as she watched, a door slid open and he started crawling out. A guard behind him.

Meghan leaped from cover, Beth following.

The two of them clubbed the hoods behind them.

The ones at the door turned. One of them dove at his weapon. Beth kicked him in the face and clobbered the other.

She attempted to kick the door down. It resisted. She pounded at the clay wall. It held firm. Her tee caught fire.

Meghan hugged her from behind and extinguished it.

They turned to the hole in the wall, through which the guard was crawling out.

They grabbed him by his feet, kicking and yelling, and knocked him out.

'Follow me,' Meghan ordered and ducked inside the hole.

# Chapter 36

It was small. It was claustrophobic. It was their only escape route.

Meghan scrabbled along earth, nails breaking, as she tried to move as fast as possible.

Beth was close behind, her panting audible, the two of them doubled over, almost hugging the ground.

Dang was a few feet ahead. Swearing, cursing, as he crawled fast.

*It's his escape route.*

He heard them and tried to move fast.

'Old,' he panted. 'It's old. Traps. It can't hold all of us. Go back.'

They didn't.

*Does he mean the VC traps are still here? It certainly looks disused.*

Meghan stopped for a moment. They didn't want to be impaled by pungi sticks.

*But he's the only one who knows all that happened. He's our witness. Besides, he's in front. We'll be safe behind him. But we need to slow him down, or else he'll get away.*

She set off, stretched out, and grabbed at his leg, which was within touching distance.

Dang cried out and kicked back. Her hand slipped.

Beth pushed her butt from behind and she sprawled forward.

Got purchase on Dang's leg and started pulling him back.

'Slow dow—'

Dang twisted and, in an acrobatic feat, turned around like an eel and attacked her with hands and feet.

She fell back.

He used the opportunity to move ahead.

She followed.

Earth fell, far ahead.

Dang yelled in alarm.

'It's falling.'

He started backtracking. Meghan reversed.

'Back,' she warned her sister.

Dang lashed out when he got near her. She ducked, but it still connected with her neck, her eyes instinctively closing.

She felt winded, and when someone screamed, a sound that echoed and curdled the blood, she thought for a moment that it had slipped out of her.

*He didn't hit me that hard.*

'God!' Beth breathed behind her, and when she peered through the dark, she swallowed.

Three bamboo poles stuck out of Dang, from his belly through his back, piercing flesh and bone.

His violent movement had triggered a trap that had survived the war and all the years afterward.

Meghan's insides twisted. No one, not even Dang, deserved to die like that.

She reached forward to help him, and then the tunnel collapsed just in front of Dang. Mud started raining on them. A small stream that thickened as the old walls and roof started giving way.

'Back,' Beth growled and yanked her.

They hadn't made it far from the lab, but it felt like miles.

Dang howling and pleading, lumps of clay falling steadily on them, around them, her elbows bleeding, and then Beth was pulling her inside the lab, shutting the trapdoor behind.

It wasn't any better in the lab.

Thick smoke choked them, tore at their eyes and burned through their lungs. Flames danced evilly, spreading heat. They couldn't see anything.

Meghan reached for Beth, a shapeless form beside her, grabbing her hand and moving to the door.

She had hardly taken a couple of steps when she doubled up, gasping, tears streaming down her face, her lungs forcing her to suck air. Smoke rushed inside them as they breathed, swamping their bodies, smothering her.

*We'll die here. No more Zeb. No more Bwana. No more Rog and his jokes.*

She sank to the floor, dragging Beth down, hoping there would be cleaner air at the bottom. There wasn't.

She started crawling. Each step was an effort. The urge to live was being snuffed out slowly by fire and smoke, which didn't care who lived or who died.

Something crashed. *Must be the wall*, she thought dully, the still-functioning part of her brain knowing her systems were shutting down.

Shadows moved.

*The guards*. She raised a leaden arm, trying to ward off an attack.

Someone grabbed at her easily, lifted her as if she weighed nothing.

'Your cavalry, ma'am. To your rescue,' said a cheerful voice, and then she passed out.

# Chapter 37

Kirilov reached the forest late.

He had been watching the hotel. He had spotted Bwana and Roger, lounging in their vehicles, and had smirked at the thought of easily taking them out.

He let that pass. They weren't his target. He still hadn't spotted Carter, but was increasingly certain he too was in Vietnam.

And then he had seen those men come out with two rolled-up carpets.

He knew immediately who was inside those carpets. An upscale hotel such as that one would never allow any maintenance men to leave through its front.

They had gone to a white van and carefully placed the two rolls inside. Further confirmation. Carpets got tossed into vehicles, not handled delicately.

He got an opening when the men were climbing in the front. There was pedestrian traffic around, and using the cover of two gossiping women, he went forward and planted a tracker on the bottom of the van.

He had followed the vehicle out of HCMC, and on the outskirts, his planning had come to nothing.

An accident involving a truck and two cars held him up. It had occurred after the van made it past a traffic light, but before he could do so.

Cruisers arrived and shut down traffic on all sides, until the injured could be recovered.

Kirilov didn't yell or swear. He sat silently and watched the tracker's signal move further away.

He rolled forward two hours later, by which time the tracker had disappeared.

He knew where its last position had been, somewhere deep in the jungle.

It took him another hour, after reaching the area, to find the tunnel.

The hidden entrance was partly open, and that helped in locating it.

He observed it from the cover of thick foliage, not moving, not making a sound.

The jungle was as silent as forests were. Birds chirped, water faintly slapped against banks, and animals scurried as they went about their business.

No sign of humans.

He approached the opening cautiously and jumped when the ground rumbled. Earthquake? No, this wasn't earthquake country.

He opened the door fully and snuck a glance in.

Darkness assailed him.

He thought of going down, when the ground shook again and he thought he smelled smoke.

He retreated to his cover and waited. Whatever was happening was in the tunnels. Someone would come out, and then Kirilov would pounce.

Zeb was way behind Kirilov and had experienced the same holdups, but magnified manyfold.

He hadn't seen the carpet rolls because of pedestrian traffic, but he had observed the Russian following the van.

He'd followed and then gotten sucked into slow-moving single-lane traffic and detours. By the time he got back on the road the Russian had been following, several hours had passed.

Something nagged at him. Why would the Russian leave the hotel?

He turned on his screen, and then he knew.

The sisters were on the move, in the jungle. Bwana and Roger were on the move too.

And then the signals disappeared.

He raced through HCMC, flouting all traffic rules. He ran red lights, passed other cars on the wrong side, his foot firmly stamped on the accelerator.

In the jungle, he slowed.

He ghosted from tree to tree, crawled where needed, and when he reached the area of last signal, he stopped.

A clearing in front of him. In shadow, sunlight reaching only in thin rays and streaks.

Something uneven about the ground.

He raised his binos carefully. Something straight-edged jutting from the ground. A door. Broken soil around it as if it had recently been forcibly widened. Significantly enlarged.

*A tunnel entrance!*

He made to rise. Something held him back.

He scanned the forest, made sure the whites of his eyes didn't show.

Spotted nothing. But that feeling didn't return.

He felt the ground shake. Fear gripped him. He recognized it immediately for what it was.

He had been in a cartel tunnel in Mexico a few missions ago. That tunnel had collapsed. He knew how that sounded.

He wanted to rise, rush to the opening and drop down.

But his inner radar held him back. There was someone or something in the jungle. Definitely not a friend.

*If Bwana and Rog are down, Beth and Meg will be safe. Those two will stop a nuclear war to save the twins. Or start one.*

He waited. He suspected Kirilov was watching too. If he moved, if he showed himself, the Russian would act.

*Let him make the first move*.

He quelled his anxiety, willing his body to remain motionless, drawing his chi inwards.

The ground shook several times. Smoke emerged from the hole.

And then he heard voices. A black hand emerged. Bwana's head followed. His friend got out with difficulty, leaned inside, and hauled Meghan out. Unconscious, but breathing. He laid her on the ground, turned back to the tunnel and pulled Beth out.

Roger climbed out last.

The two men picked up the sisters as if they weighed nothing and set off at a run.

The earth groaned, loose mud trembled and got sucked into the hole.

And still, Zeb didn't move.

Sweat beaded down his face, his heart beat slowly. The sisters were alive. He showed no trace of emotion, however. He felt cold, empty.

He was waiting for Kirilov.

Minutes felt like hours.

Birds chattered. A snake slithered a few feet in front of him.

Still no sign of the Russian. No trace of anyone.

He was turning his head a fraction when he felt it. Something approaching fast.

Something struck him hard on his left temple, so hard that it left him stunned.

He was rolling even as he had sensed the motion, and that saved him.

He rose to his feet swiftly.

Kirilov! He was there, in front of him, in a black shirt, dark trousers. His hands were empty, his eyes were dark holes.

'I don't need guns to take you out,' he said, reading Zeb's mind.

'No. You're scared my friends will hear any shots and come back to investigate,' Zeb taunted in Russian.

'Your friends. I could have taken them out just then. I didn't. I knew you were here somewhere. I can always find them.'

He attacked without warning. Coming in fast, hands whirling.

Zeb knew several fighting styles. He had learned various arts in the East and the West. If he had to pick the deadliest form of combat, it would be Krav Maga, used by the Israeli Defense Forces. There was no spirituality to be attained in that style, no harmony to be reached.

It was designed to inflict maximum damage on an opponent.

The Russian turned out to be an expert in that school of fighting.

Zeb was on the backfoot, evading Kirilov's blows and thrusts.

He used his elbows and feet to block and parry, no time to go on the offense.

And still his assailant came, as if having an endless supply of breath.

Each punch felt like a hammer, numbing Zeb's body.

He tripped on a root, fell, and turned swiftly to escape the incoming knee.

Kirilov laughed and held back.

Zeb didn't rise.

He spun on his back and kicked the Russian's legs from under him.

That was the intent. It didn't go down like he wanted.

His attacker's limbs felt like concrete, and when Zeb gasped and stopped moving for a fractional second, he was hauled up, and the trip-hammers rained down on him.

On his ribs. On his face. On his eyes.

His hands came up defensively, ineffectively. The Russian's thumb searched his face to gouge his eyes.

And then Zeb snapped.

He headbutted the Russian. Cold heat raced through him. He used Cham's broken body and sobbing to fuel his anger.

The memory of the unconscious sisters to channel it.

Zeb wasn't going to die that day. Not in the forest. Not while his friends were alive.

Kirilov was pounding him, one hand around his tee to hold him, the other to punch him.

Zeb soaked it in. Detached mind from body. Pain was nothing. It could be boxed. Like those memories of his.

Once it was dealt with, the body was nothing but flesh,

bones, and sinew. What was the worst that could happen?

Zeb's right fist curled and bunched.

His knuckles jutted out.

Even as he trembled under the force of the attack, he counterpunched.

Hard, between Kirilov's ribs.

He traded blow for blow. The two men breathing harshly, standing close, as if embracing, their hands moving robotically, bodies shuddering under the impact.

Zeb didn't exist. The forest was a bleak darkness. All that mattered was repeatedly landing his knuckles in the same spot, in between Kirilov's ribs.

He didn't know how long he kept hitting. How long he kept punching. The beast had taken over.

And then he felt the grip around him loosen.

Still, he persisted. Felt ribs crack beneath his punches. Felt groans escape the Russian.

He didn't let up. He would die, but he wouldn't give in.

Kirilov fell. Zeb fell on top. His right hand kept punching until liquid poured out and his fingers scraped bone.

Zeb was beyond hearing. Beyond reasoning.

And when his body gave up, no energy left, he turned his head slowly and discovered the Russian was beyond breathing.

Zeb fell back, staring at the canopy above him. He closed his eyes, and he must have passed out, because when he opened them, it was dark.

He got to his feet slowly.

Dragged Kirilov's body to the tunnel.

Shoved it with difficulty inside the hole.

Fumbled at his backpack, removed two detonators, and tossed them in behind the body.

He took off at a stumbling run towards the river.

The shock of the water brought everything back. The world started turning on its axis again. And with it came pain, searing fire that burned through him.

He lay on his back, floating in the water, gasping in agony.

Pain was good. It meant he was alive.

And when he thought of Beth and Meghan's smiles, his body started warming.

# Chapter 38

Roger was driving the next day, Meghan beside him, Bwana and Beth at the rear.

They were heading back to the airport. Back to their country.

They had been through the wringer the previous evening.

They had rushed the sisters to a private hospital, where the twins had been thoroughly examined.

They had spent hours in the lobby, pacing, not conversing. People had given them a wide berth, as if sensing the darkness within them. Zeb didn't return their calls, but that wasn't concerning. Their friend frequently dropped off the radar.

They cracked smiles only when the white-coated medics told them the twins would be fine. There wasn't anything permanently damaged. Their lungs and airways were fine. Sure, they had inhaled smoke, lots of it, but the hospital had given them oxygen.

Were they awake?

See for yourself, the medics had said.

They barged into the Petersens' room and when they saw their smiles, it was sunlight.

'What happened?' Bwana asked, concealing his delight.

'Dang's dead. Josh Patten is alive.' Beth told them everything.

Neither she nor Meghan put up any fight when Roger declared they were returning to the US.

There was nothing more to be done in Vietnam. They called Colonel General Lanh, explained everything, and waited for him to explode at them.

Lanh didn't. He was delighted. Dang was dead? That was one less criminal. It didn't matter that there was no proof. He believed the sisters. The tunnels had collapsed? Even better. He would check out that area of the jungle. Close it off to the public and seal it.

'I'll handle everything,' he told them. He had conducted his own discreet investigation ever since the ads had run. He had discovered there was more than sufficient reason to believe that the man posing as Nang Quy Dang was indeed a master criminal. There was the small matter of proof, but now, that was no longer required.

'You never told us how you both happened to be there. In the jungle.' Beth leaned sideways so that she could watch Roger.

'Coincidence.' The Texan grinned as he overtook a car that was defying Vietnam's unwritten traffic rules. It was going slow. 'Sheer, dumb luck. Bwana and I were on one of our camping trips. Just happened that we were right there. We heard this ground shaking. Decided to investigate. Our jaws dropped when we came across the two of you.'

'You expect us to believe that?'

'My mama raised me never to tell lies,' Roger replied, straight-faced.

'You don't know who your mama is.' Beth snorted. 'You're forgetting we know your story. You were raised in a foster home. Not the best folks, from what I recall.'

'Ungrateful,' Bwana came to his friend's rescue. 'That's the word, isn't it, Rog?'

'It sure is,' Roger replied in an injured tone. 'We risked life and limb to save these two. We even ended our vacation. And what do we get in return?'

'The third degree.' Bwana nodded in agreement. 'You hear those magic words, Rog? Thank you?'

'Nope. It must be my hearing, 'cause surely these nice sweet women would have said them words a million times.'

He swerved suddenly, to a chorus of horns from behind.

He straightened, raised a hand in apology, and wiped his cheek where Beth had kissed him.

He didn't stop smiling all the way to the airport.

Beth and Meghan met Cole Patten in his office in New York a week later.

Ken Farrell was in attendance, both men dressed in suits, seated comfortably in leather chairs.

'You returned from Vietnam sometime back. You didn't return my calls or emails. You're meeting us only now?' Patten questioned them.

'There were a few matters we had to attend to.' Beth dropped into a chair and crossed her legs while Meghan went to a picture window and leaned against it.

'Something more important than briefing us?'

'Yeah.'

'Like—'

'Like calling plastic surgeons around the country, and a

few around the world, too. You don't know this, but there are several surgeons who cooperate with us. It's all those pesky terrorists and criminals. They keep altering their faces. Those of us hunting them never know what they look like. So, we befriended the best, the most discreet surgeons. Threw the book at them. Promised them prison time if they didn't cooperate. Now, almost all of them do.'

Patten spread his hands helplessly. 'Are you going somewhere with this?'

'We met Dang in Vietnam,' Meghan broke in.

Both men turned to her.

'He was an international criminal. A drug runner. A former North Vietnamese soldier. Your father was his partner.'

'Whoa.' Patten reared back as if stung. 'That's a lot to take in.'

'Relax, Cole,' Farrell interjected. 'That's your father, not you. Let's hear them out.'

Meghan broke it down for them, going into every detail, except Dang's revelation about Josh.

The two men hung on to her every word, fascinated, and moved only when she had finished.

'I don't know what to think,' Patten mumbled, raking his fingers through his hair. 'I always thought Dad was a hero. All this…it's hard to digest. Dang could have been lying.'

'He wasn't. There was no reason to.'

'The Vietnamese police let you go, just like that?'

'Yeah.'

'I find that hard to believe.'

'Believe what you want,' Meghan replied brusquely.

'None of this can leak,' Farrell injected smoothly before his client could take offense. 'Cole is already under pressure.

None of this can be proven, and there's no reason for these developments to be in the open.'

'Relax, how crooked Billy Patten was isn't of interest to us.'

'What was that about plastic surgeons?' The lawyer's gaze sharpened.

'Glad you brought that up,' Beth drawled, 'but before we get to that, there's one more matter.'

'We went to the nursing home. Leroy Duhan's.' Meghan hitched a leg and made herself comfortable against the window. She was enjoying herself and didn't hide it. 'You know what we found?'

'Your client, Cole Patten, visited it some months back. We matched the visit against our timeline. It was just after Gorbunov made his allegations that your client wasn't who he was.'

'Thing is,' Beth said, smiling slowly like a wolf ready to pounce, 'you told us you'd never met Duhan or Garrett or any of your father's friends.'

Meghan rummaged through her bag, pulled out a folder and tossed it at Farrell. 'Surveillance video images of your client entering the nursing home. There's a visitor log with his name on it.'

Farrell threw a shocked glance at his client, whose face had turned grey.

'There's more,' she said, twisting the knife. 'Those plastic surgeons Beth was talking about.

'One of them, in Brazil, confirmed your client had his scar removed. This was after he became CEO of Chisholm.'

'And that's not all.' Beth dropped the bombshell. 'Dang said Billy Patten's last words were *Josh, run away*. It was Josh

Patten who escaped. Not Cole Patten. Your client is a fake.'

'That's a lie.' Patten rose out of his chair furiously. 'Ken, these two are slandering me. We need to—'

The doors burst open and two men walked in. One was as immaculately turned out as Patten, the other sleepy-eyed and in a rumpled white suit.

Patten's EA followed them, her face distressed.

'You need to come with us, Mr. Patten,' the man in the front finished for the billionaire.'

'And you are?' Farrell asked when he had recovered.

'Pizaka, sir, and my partner, Chang. NYPD. We're senior detectives with a task force reporting directly to the commissioner.'

'You can't arrest me,' Patten cried, stumbling back. 'Ken, do something.'

'We aren't arresting your client, Mr. Farrell. We want to question him.' Pizaka didn't bat an eyelid. Not that they could see anything of his eyes. They were concealed behind his ever-present shades. 'You're welcome to accompany him.'

'I will,' Ken Farrell replied stiffly.

'You were supposed to prove I'm Cole Patten. I'll sue you,' Patten yelled shrilly. His poise had deserted him. His eyes were wild, his face flushed, as his lawyer placed a hand behind his back and urged him towards the door.

'Nope,' Meghan replied, unable to keep the smirk off her face. 'We said we would find out who you were.'

She winked at Chang as the cops left with the lawyer and his client.

'Case closed?' Beth asked her.

'Yeah.' She high-fived her sister. 'Very satisfyingly.'

It wasn't for Zeb. He had one call to make.

Gorbunov didn't react when he walked into the Russian's office and slipped into a chair.

The mafia boss didn't ask how he had evaded the security and his secretarial desk.

'You know who I am?'

'*Da*.' His eyes searched behind Zeb's back.

'He isn't coming. Kirilov.'

The gang boss's eyes narrowed. The skin on his face stretched.

'He's in Vietnam. In a tunnel. He will never return.'

A soft voice was speaking rapidly in the background. A reporter on the wall-mounted TV. She was covering the developments at Chisholm Corporation. Its share price had sunk to a new low following Patten's questioning by the NYPD. Rumors swirled thick and fast that Cole Patten was really Josh Patten. The NYPD had yet to confirm. Patten's lawyer was tight-lipped.

'It won't do you any good,' Zeb commented, glancing at the TV.

The Russian blinked, his fists flexed.

'Why?'

Zeb raised his wrist and glanced at his watch.

'Because you'll be dead in five minutes.'

Zeb was snoozing on his couch a full week later. He wasn't fully recovered. His body was a walking wound. Two cracked ribs were healing slowly. Numerous cuts and lacerations were mending. However, he concealed his injuries from his friends. He was a master of disguise and even hid the bruises on his face.

The sisters had brought him up to speed on Patten, who was now under investigation, and on the events in Vietnam.

Gorbunov's death was a mystery. The cops had no clues. Massive heart attack, the coroner said, and that was what the NYPD went with. The media went to town, speculating that rival gangs had somehow killed the Russian.

Their office returned to normalcy. There wasn't anything urgent, no missions, no active operations. Beth spent more time with Mark and was often away.

Meghan stayed till late that evening, completing orders for new SUVs. They had decided to have more vehicles in different cities, and that meant garages had to be identified and arrangements had to be made.

She glanced at the man on the couch.

'Zeb?'

'Hmm?'

'You were in Vietnam, weren't you?'

His eyes shot open. 'Nope. Was getting acquainted with this couch. Whatever gave you that idea?'

She gave him a measured look. 'You know of someone called Kirilov?'

'Never heard of him. Who's he?'

'Bwana and Rog. They were talking about him when they thought they were alone.'

'You spied on them?'

'I didn't.' She smiled slyly. 'I just didn't let on that I was there.'

'Who is he?'

'Gorbunov's killer. No one knows of him. No photographs, nothing in any police dossier. He doesn't exist.'

'What's that got to do with me?'

'Bwana and Rog again. They think he doesn't exist anymore. You took care of him.'

'I was here all along.'

'Here's the thing, Zeb. Your GPS trail. Your tracker says you returned from the Middle East, when we were away. It shows you were in New York ever since. However, I ran some fancy programs on it. Nothing you would understand. And those show that you faked the signal. You returned a while back. Before we went to Vietnam.'

'So, where was I?'

She shrugged. 'Those programs didn't tell me that. But I know.' Her green eyes pinned him down. 'You returned early from your mission. Kept away to see if any badasses had followed you. And then, you followed us to Vietnam. You got Bwana and Rog to trail us, but you were there too.'

'You've been watching too many movies, Meg.' He rose, yawned, and stretched.

'Your life, what you do…Hollywood doesn't even come close.' No smile crossed her face. Just that steady look.

Zeb retied his laces and started heading to the door.

'Gorbunov,' she said, and he stopped.

'You turned off your tracker for a few hours. Coincidentally, the Russian died that day, in the interval your GPS signal disappeared. Your device's last position was a block away from the Russian's office.'

'I know you killed him.'

'I didn't,' he laughed. 'I don't go around killing gangsters for no reason.'

'Except that there was a reason. Kirilov was Gorbunov's man. I think he sent his killer after us in Vietnam.'

'You're overthinking this,' he told her solicitously and

strode out.

'Zeb,' she called, stopping him again, and he turned around with an audible sigh.

'I would have done the same. In your position.'

She smiled, and sunlight began.

**Coming soon**

# RUN!

Warriors Series, Book 12

By

Ty Patterson

# Bonus Chapter from ***RUN!***

He came from Beirut. He came from war. His name was Waleed Khalid Bilal, but not many remembered that name. Namir was what everyone called him. Those who feared him, and there were many of them, and those who respected him as well.

Namir. Leopard.

They had started calling him that because of his ability to strike without warning and disappear into nothingness.

No one knew when and where he would come from. All knew that when he left, there would be death and destruction behind him.

The name had originated in a small village in the Bekaa Valley of Lebanon.

He and his small band of men had ambushed and captured an American convoy of thirty. He had killed most of them and, after torturing five of them, had left them to die in the heat.

Namir. That's when his men had started calling him by that name.

Namir had known war all his life. He was born during a Lebanese army bombing raid in the valley. His parents died in the attack, and Namir grew up an orphan, reared by neighbors and militants. The first object he recalled holding in his hands was an AK-47.

His first kill was when he was eight years old.

It wasn't planned. His gun went off when he was playing with it and killed an old villager.

He fled the place and joined a wandering band of armed militants. War became not just his solace, but his profession.

The militants Namir had joined were a splinter group of Hezbollah, who themselves waged a political and terrorist war against Israel and America and also persecuted people of other faiths.

Namir grew up in that toxic environment and quickly found he was better at military strategy than any other militant in his group. And that he liked killing and torture.

He killed the leader of his group when he was twenty-five. The splinter cell was fifty strong at that time and had total control of a small village in the Bekaa Valley, a hundred miles north of Beirut, high up in the Anti-Lebanon Mountains.

The village, with two hundred residents, was once famous for its handmade carpets.

Now, as with most of the valley, it was better known for its hashish fields.

Namir's gang controlled hundreds of acres of such fields, the villagers effectively serving the bandits. Hashish sales, however, were being rapidly overtaken by the manufacture of Captagon, an addictive drug that helped fighters stay awake for days and fight like zombies.

Namir had converted four houses in the village into laboratories, the hub of his multimillion-dollar income.

It was when he turned thirty-five that it came crashing down on him.

He was returning from Beirut, where he and his men had killed twenty Christians after raping their women.

They had done nothing to Namir or his gang. They were in a church, praying, while the militants had been returning after fighting the Lebanese army.

It had started raining, and their open-topped Jeeps didn't offer much cover.

They took cover in the church, whose occupants ordered them to leave.

Namir, high on Captagon, was in no mood to obey. He slapped the nearest man, at which several other rushed at him.

In no time, their AKs slipped into their hands, and a few minutes later, several innocents were dead.

'We can have some fun.' One militant grinned, looking in the direction of the cowering women.'

'Yes,' Namir agreed.

Unknown to him, one man had gotten away from the massacre. Kenton Ashland, an American reporter.

Ashland had been in the church and had fled as soon as the militants arrived.

He had heard the sounds of firing and had crept back cautiously.

He hid underneath a vehicle that was parked in front of the wide-open doors. What he saw sickened him, and he started recording it on his cell.

He uploaded the video to the Internet, after which events moved quickly.

There were American forces in Beirut, based close to the church. They were alerted by the Lebanese police, who had put a time and location stamp on the footage, and when Namir set out two hours later, the trap was ready, waiting.

The militants' capture was widely covered by international media, and Namir was branded as a war criminal.

He was tried, amidst global publicity, in the Special Tribunal for Lebanon, in the Netherlands. He was convicted and sentenced to fifteen years in prison.

He was transported back to Lebanon and began his jail time in Beirut.

However, he didn't serve his full term.

A month after his fortieth birthday, his militants organized a full-scale attack on the prison, supported by many other gangs.

Namir escaped, along with several other prisoners.

He fled the country on a private plane after being provided with a fake passport and papers.

He went to Switzerland, drew sufficient amounts of money from his private accounts and, using yet another passport, he flew to America.

Namir had a long memory. Coupled with that, he had an unforgiving nature.

It was time to pay Kenton Ashland a visit.

And bring war to anyone who stood in Namir's way.

# Author's Message

Thank you for taking the time to read *I Am Missing*. If you enjoyed it, please consider telling your friends and posting a short review.

Sign up to Ty Patterson's mailing list and get The Warrior, #1 in the USA Today Bestselling Warriors Series, free. Be the first to know about new releases and deals.

Check out Ty on Amazon, on iTunes, on Kobo, on Google Play, and on Barnes and Noble.

## Books by Ty Patterson

Warriors Series Shorts

*This is a series of novellas that link to the Warriors Series thrillers*

*Zulu Hour*, Warriors Series Shorts, Book 1 (set before *The Warrior*)
*The Watcher*, Warriors Series Shorts, Book 2 (set between *The Warrior* and *The Warrior Code*)
*The Shadow*, Warriors Series Shorts, Book 3 (set before *The Warrior*)
*The Man From Congo*, Warriors Series Shorts, Book 4
Warriors Series Shorts, Boxset I, Books 1-4
*The Texan*, Warriors Series Shorts, Book 5
*The Heavies*, Warriors Series Shorts, Book 6

Gemini Series

*Dividing Zero*, Gemini Series, Book 1
*Defending Cain*, Gemini Series, Book 2
*I Am Missing*, Gemini Series, Book 3

Warriors Series

*The Warrior*, Warriors series, Book 1
*The Reluctant Warrior*, Warriors series, Book 2
*The Warrior Code*, Warriors series, Book 3
*The Warrior's Debt*, Warriors series, Book 4
*Flay*, Warriors series, Book 5
*Behind You*, Warriors series, Book 6
*Hunting You*, Warriors series, Book 7
*Zero*, Warriors series, Book 8
*Death Club*, Warriors series, Book 9
*Trigger Break*, Warriors series, Book 10
*Scorched Earth*, Warriors series, Book 11
*RUN!*, Warriors series, Book 12
Warriors series Boxset, Books 1-4
Warriors series Boxset II, Books 5-8
Warriors series Boxset III, Books 1-8

Sign up to Ty Patterson's mailing list, and get The Warrior, #1 in the USA Today Bestselling Warriors Series, free. Be the first to know about new releases and deals.

Check out Ty on Amazon, on iTunes, on Kobo and on Barnes and Noble.

# About the Author

Ty has lived on a couple of continents and has been a trench digger, loose tea vendor, leather goods salesman, marine lubricants salesman, diesel engine mechanic, and is now an action thriller author.

Ty is privileged that readers of crime suspense and action thrillers have loved his books. 'Intense,' 'Riveting,' and 'Gripping' have been commonly used in reviews.

Ty lives with his wife and son, who humor his ridiculous belief that he's in charge.


**Connect with Ty:**

Twitter: @pattersonty67

Facebook: www.facebook.com/AuthorTyPatterson

Website www.typatterson.com

Mailing list: www.typatterson.com/subscribe

Made in United States
North Haven, CT
10 May 2025

68742754R00166